THE ANGRY BIRDS™

BIG MOVIE
EGGSTRAVAGANZA

Become our fan on Facebook facebook.com/idwpublishing
Follow us on Twitter @idwpublishing
Subscribe to us on YouTube youtube.com/idwpublishing
See what's new on Tumblr tumblr.idwpublishing.com
Check us out on Instagram instagram.com/idwpublishing

COLLECTION EDITS BY
JUSTIN EISINGER
AND ALONZO SIMON

PUBLISHER
TED ADAMS

COLLECTION DESIGN BY
CHRIS MOWRY

Thanks to Jukka Heiskanen,
Juha Mäkinen, and the Rovio
team for their hard work and
invaluable assistance.

Rovio Books:

Mikael Hed, Executive Producer
Laura Nevanlinna, Publishing Director
Jukka Heiskanen, Editor-in-Chief, Comics
Juha Mäkinen, Editor, Comics
Henrik Sarimo, Graphic Designer
Nathan Cosby, Freelance Editor

For international rights, please
contact licensing@idwpublishing.com

ISBN: 978-1-63140-568-6

19 18 17 16   1 2 3 4

IDW Publishing:

Ted Adams, CEO & Publisher
Greg Goldstein, President & COO
Robbie Robbins, EVP/Sr. Graphic Artist
Chris Ryall, Chief Creative Officer/Editor-in-Chief
Matthew Ruzicka, CPA, Chief Financial Officer
Dirk Wood, VP of Marketing
Lorelei Bunjes, VP of Digital Services
Jeff Webber, VP of Licensing, Digital and Subsidiary Righ*
Jerry Bennington, VP of New Product Development

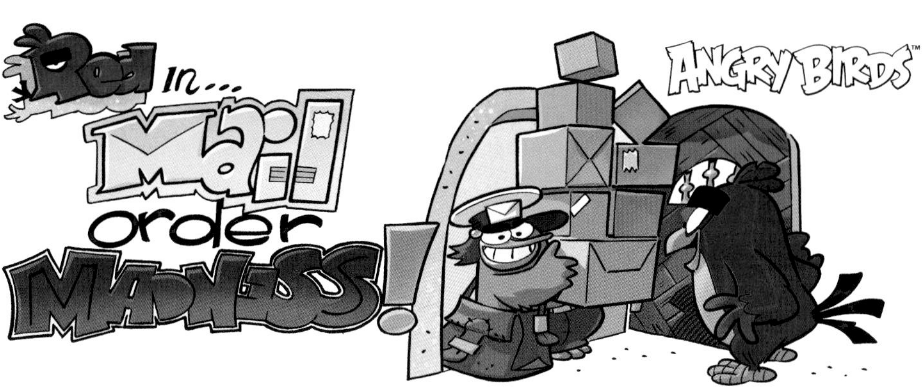
Red in...
Mail order Madness!
ANGRY BIRDS™

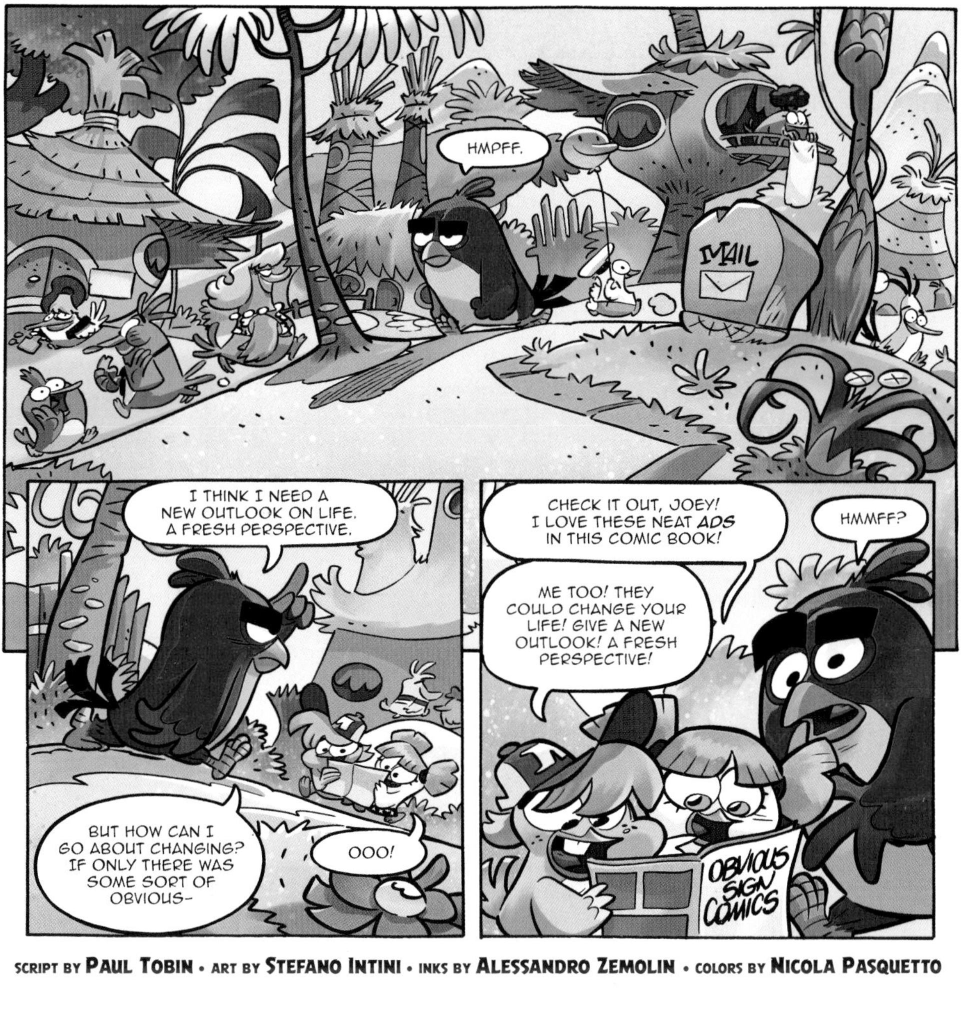
HMPFF.
MAIL
I THINK I NEED A NEW OUTLOOK ON LIFE. A FRESH PERSPECTIVE.
BUT HOW CAN I GO ABOUT CHANGING? IF ONLY THERE WAS SOME SORT OF OBVIOUS-
OOO!
CHECK IT OUT, JOEY! I LOVE THESE NEAT *ADS* IN THIS COMIC BOOK!
HMMFF?
ME TOO! THEY COULD CHANGE YOUR LIFE! GIVE A NEW OUTLOOK! A FRESH PERSPECTIVE!
OBVIOUS SIGN COMICS

SCRIPT BY **PAUL TOBIN** • ART BY **STEFANO INTINI** • INKS BY **ALESSANDRO ZEMOLIN** • COLORS BY **NICOLA PASQUETTO**

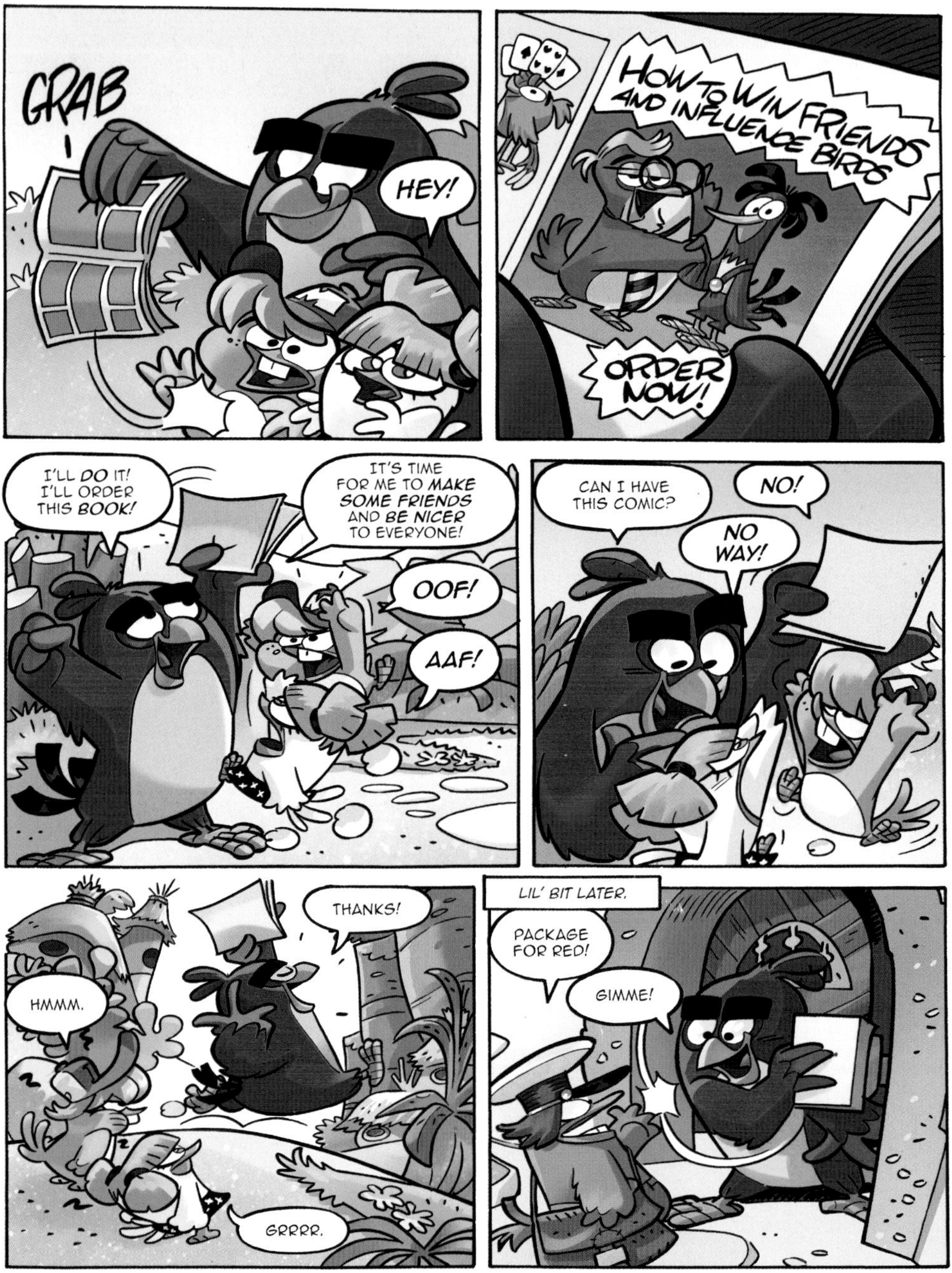
GRAB
HEY!
HOW TO WIN FRIENDS AND INFLUENCE BIRDS
ORDER NOW!
I'LL DO IT! I'LL ORDER THIS BOOK!
IT'S TIME FOR ME TO MAKE SOME FRIENDS AND BE NICER TO EVERYONE!
OOF!
AAF!
CAN I HAVE THIS COMIC?
NO!
NO WAY!
THANKS!
HMMM.
GRRRR.
LIL' BIT LATER.
PACKAGE FOR RED!
GIMME!

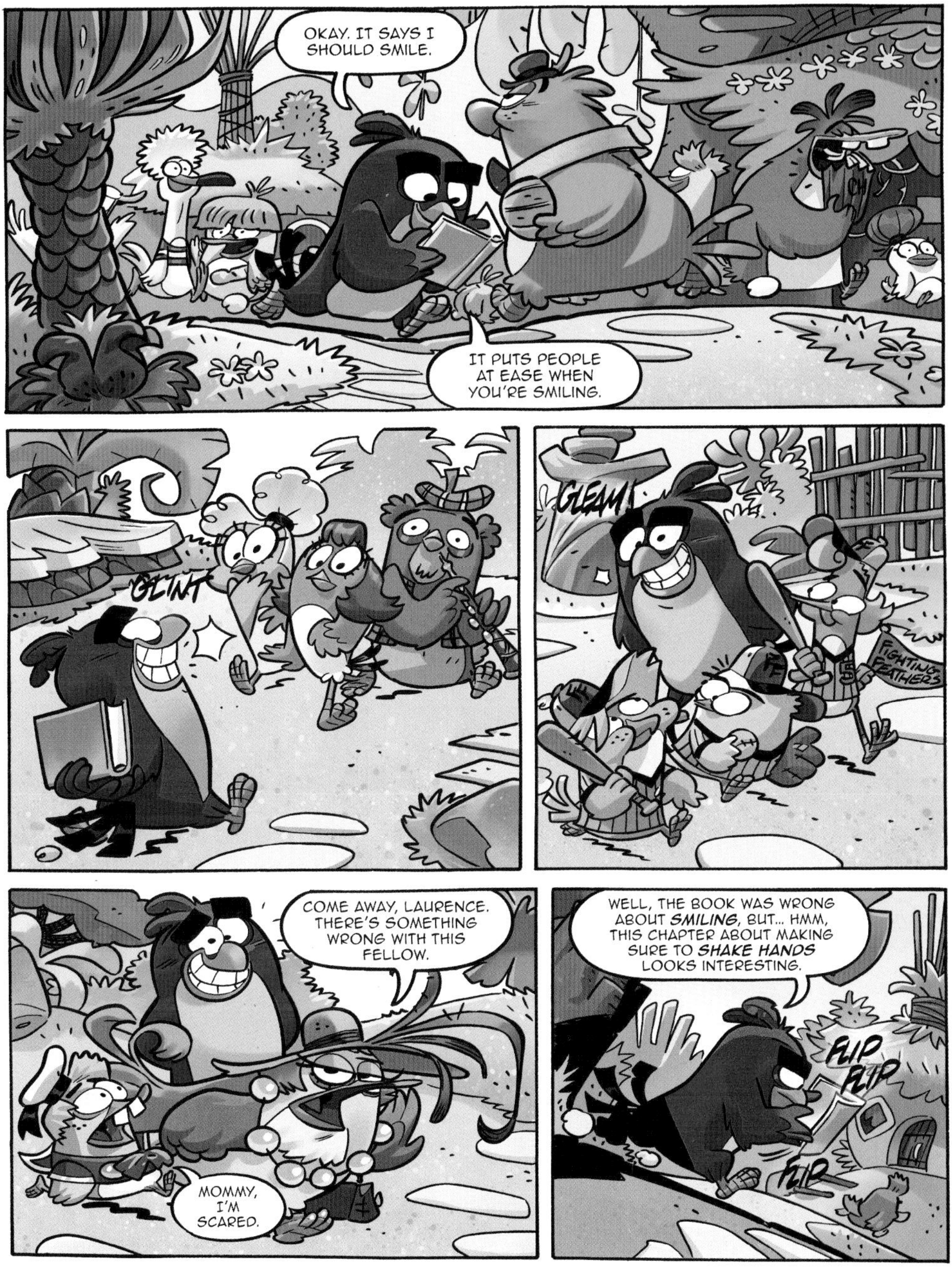
OKAY. IT SAYS I SHOULD SMILE.
IT PUTS PEOPLE AT EASE WHEN YOU'RE SMILING.
GLINT
GLEAM
FIGHTING FEATHERS
COME AWAY, LAURENCE. THERE'S SOMETHING WRONG WITH THIS FELLOW.
MOMMY, I'M SCARED.
WELL, THE BOOK WAS WRONG ABOUT SMILING, BUT... HMM, THIS CHAPTER ABOUT MAKING SURE TO SHAKE HANDS LOOKS INTERESTING.
FLIP FLIP
FLIP

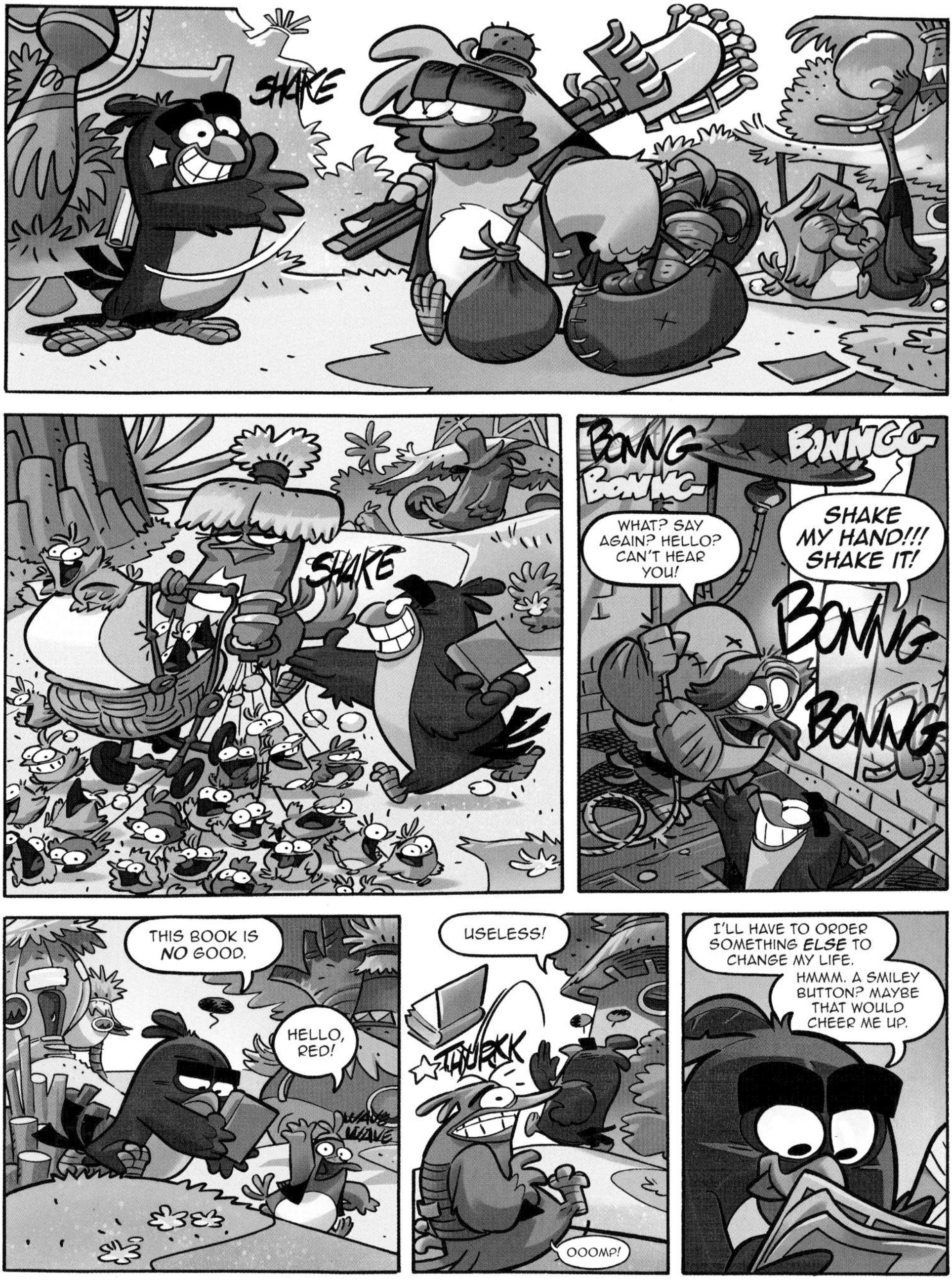

SHAKE
SHAKE
BONNG
BONNG
BONNGG
WHAT? SAY AGAIN? HELLO? CAN'T HEAR YOU!
SHAKE MY HAND!!! SHAKE IT!
BONNG
BONNG
THIS BOOK IS NO GOOD.
HELLO, RED!
WAVE WAVE
USELESS!
THURKK
OOOMP!
I'LL HAVE TO ORDER SOMETHING ELSE TO CHANGE MY LIFE.
HMMM. A SMILEY BUTTON? MAYBE THAT WOULD CHEER ME UP.

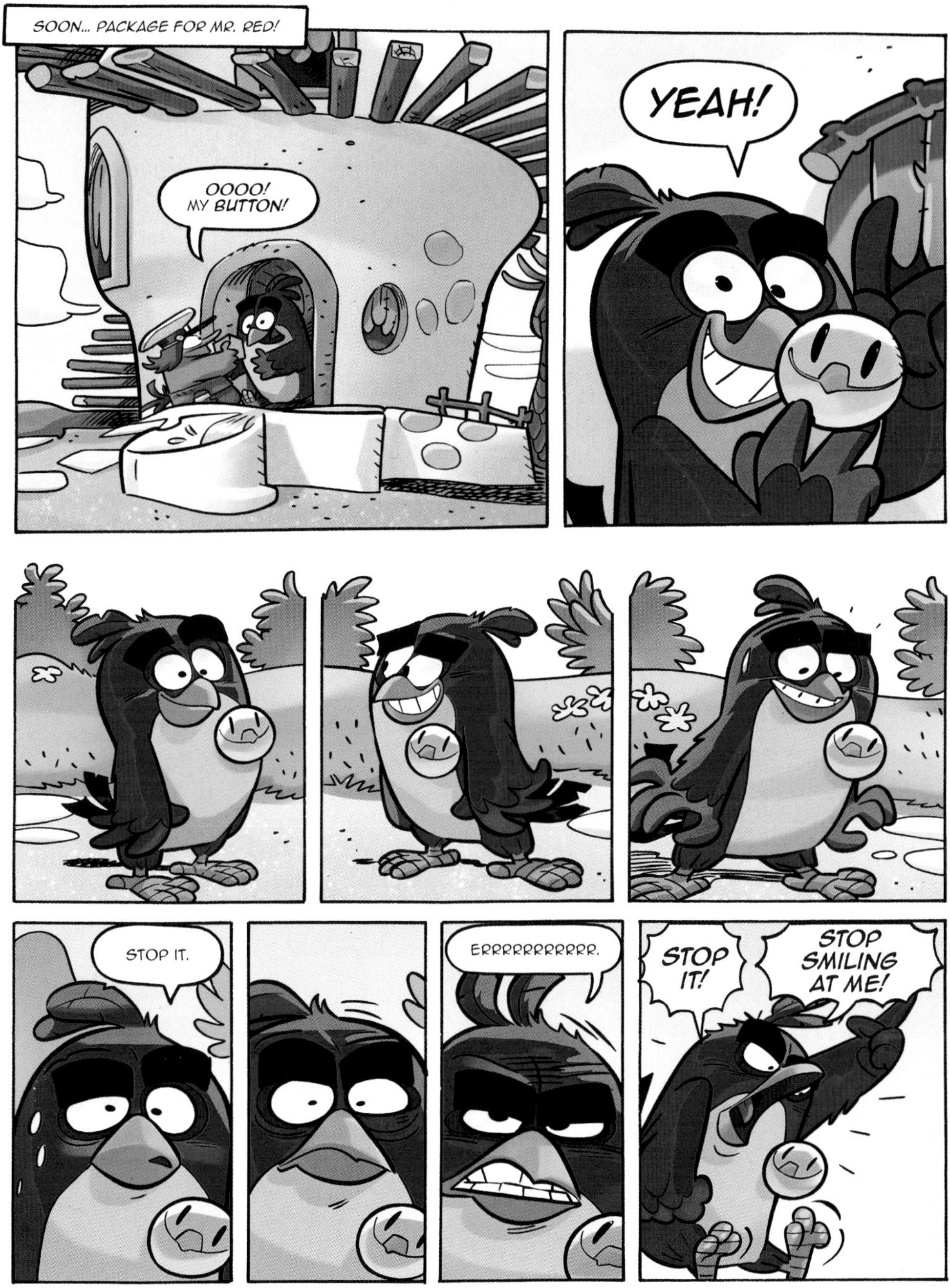
SOON... PACKAGE FOR MR. RED!
OOOO! MY BUTTON!
YEAH!
STOP IT.
ERRRRRRRRRRR.
STOP IT!
STOP SMILING AT ME!

SOON...
HA HA HA
ZAP
HA
"JOY BUZZER! BE THE LIFE OF THE PARTY"
ORDER NOW!
AND THEN...
BUZZZT
THUMP
THUMP
THUMP
THUMP
THUMP
THE BOWTIE THAT SQUIRTS WATER! MAKE EVERYONE LAUGH!
HA
HA
SPLISH!
HA
HA
GET YOURS NOW!
AND SO...
SPLORSHH!
OH!
THUMP
THUMP
THUMP
THUMP
THUMP

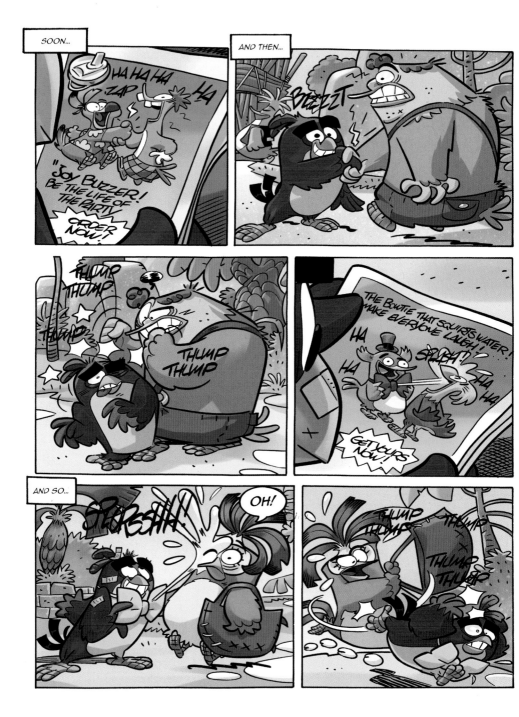

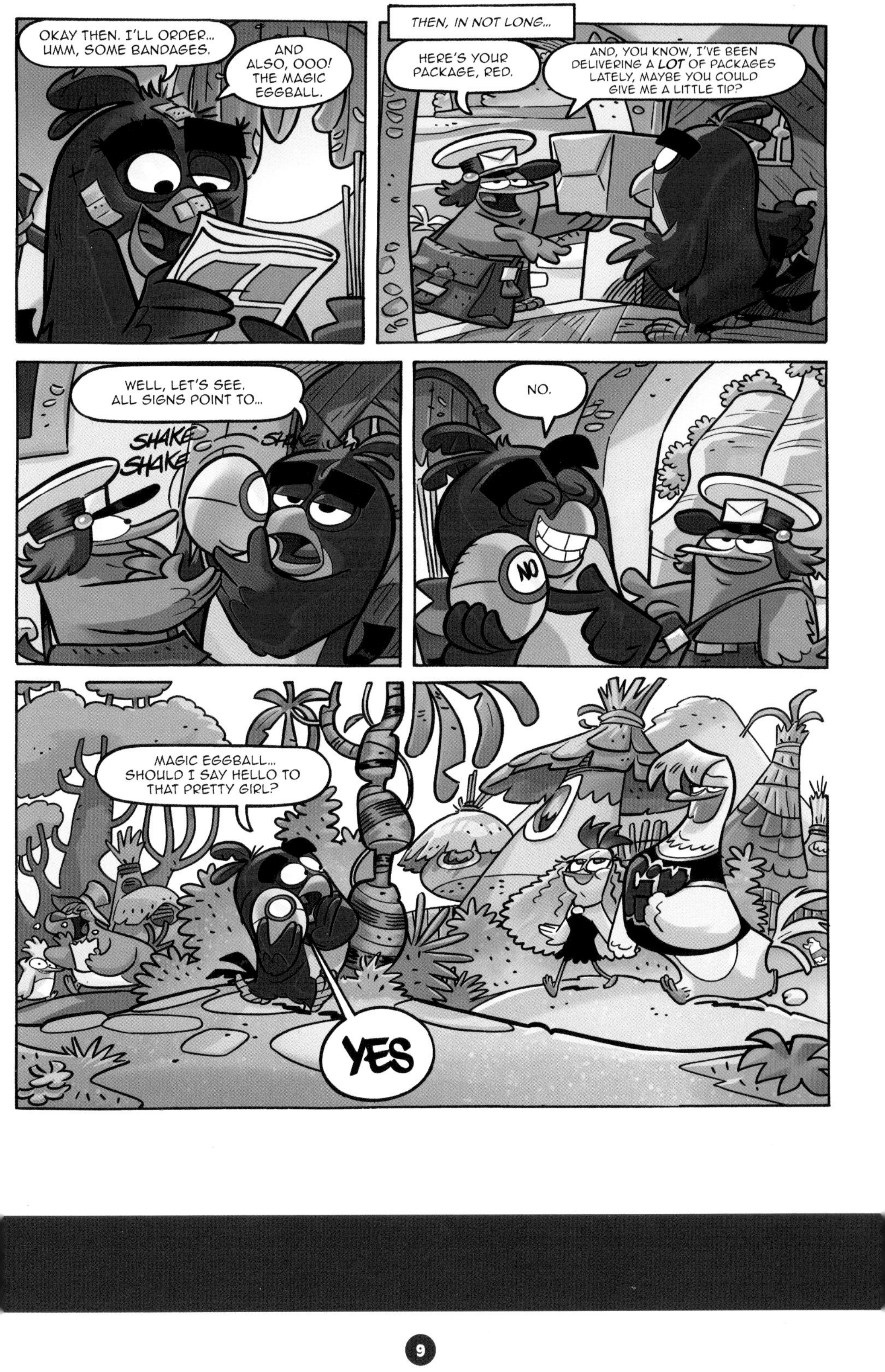
OKAY THEN. I'LL ORDER... UMM, SOME BANDAGES.
AND ALSO, OOO! THE MAGIC EGGBALL.
THEN, IN NOT LONG...
HERE'S YOUR PACKAGE, RED.
AND, YOU KNOW, I'VE BEEN DELIVERING A **LOT** OF PACKAGES LATELY, MAYBE YOU COULD GIVE ME A LITTLE TIP?
WELL, LET'S SEE. ALL SIGNS POINT TO...
SHAKE SHAKE
SHAKE
NO.
NO
MAGIC EGGBALL... SHOULD I SAY HELLO TO THAT PRETTY GIRL?
YES

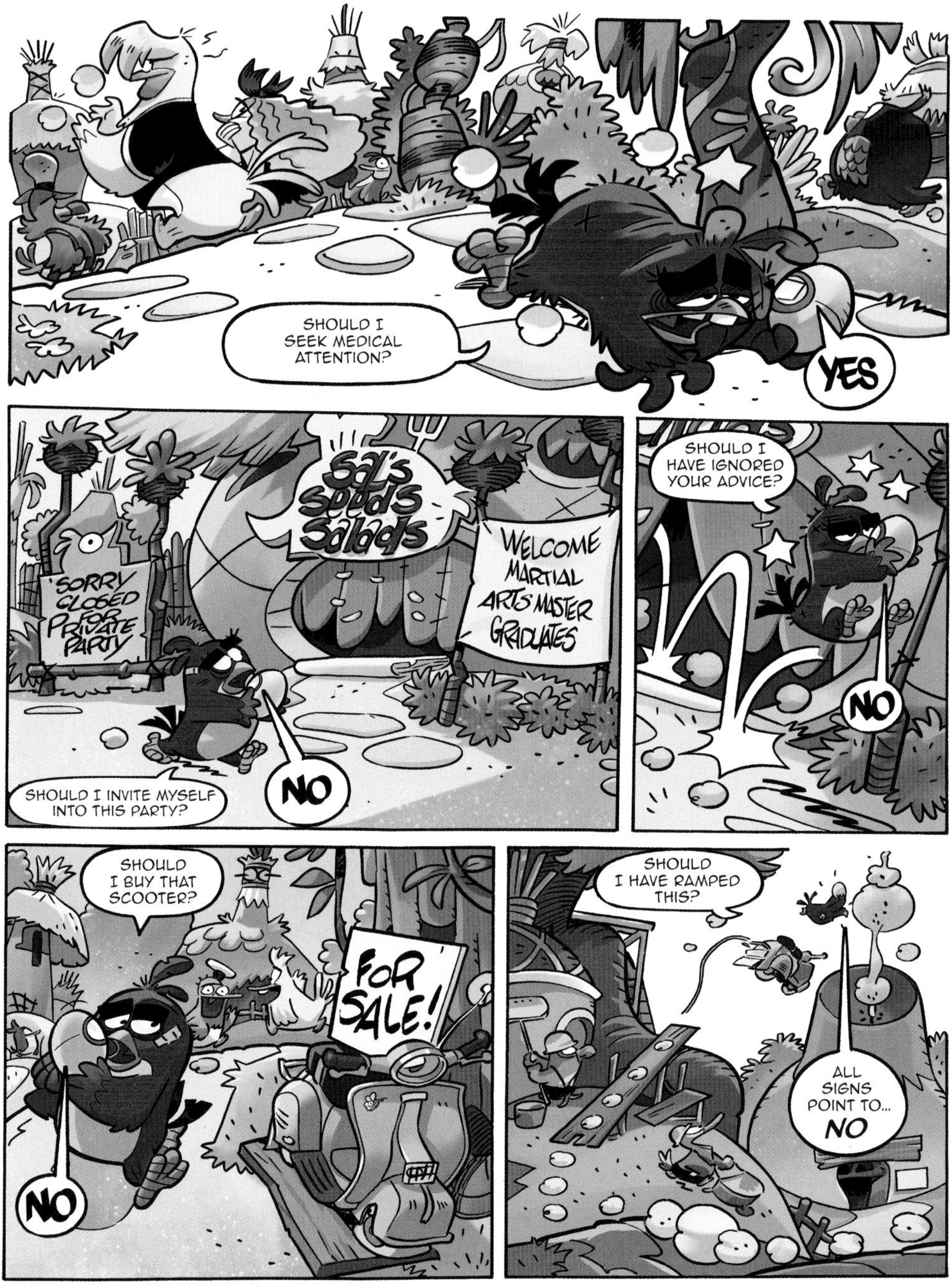
SHOULD I SEEK MEDICAL ATTENTION?
YES
SORRY CLOSED FOR PRIVATE PARTY
Sal's Seeds Salads
WELCOME MARTIAL ARTS MASTER GRADUATES
SHOULD I INVITE MYSELF INTO THIS PARTY?
NO
SHOULD I HAVE IGNORED YOUR ADVICE?
NO
SHOULD I BUY THAT SCOOTER?
FOR SALE!
NO
SHOULD I HAVE RAMPED THIS?
ALL SIGNS POINT TO... NO

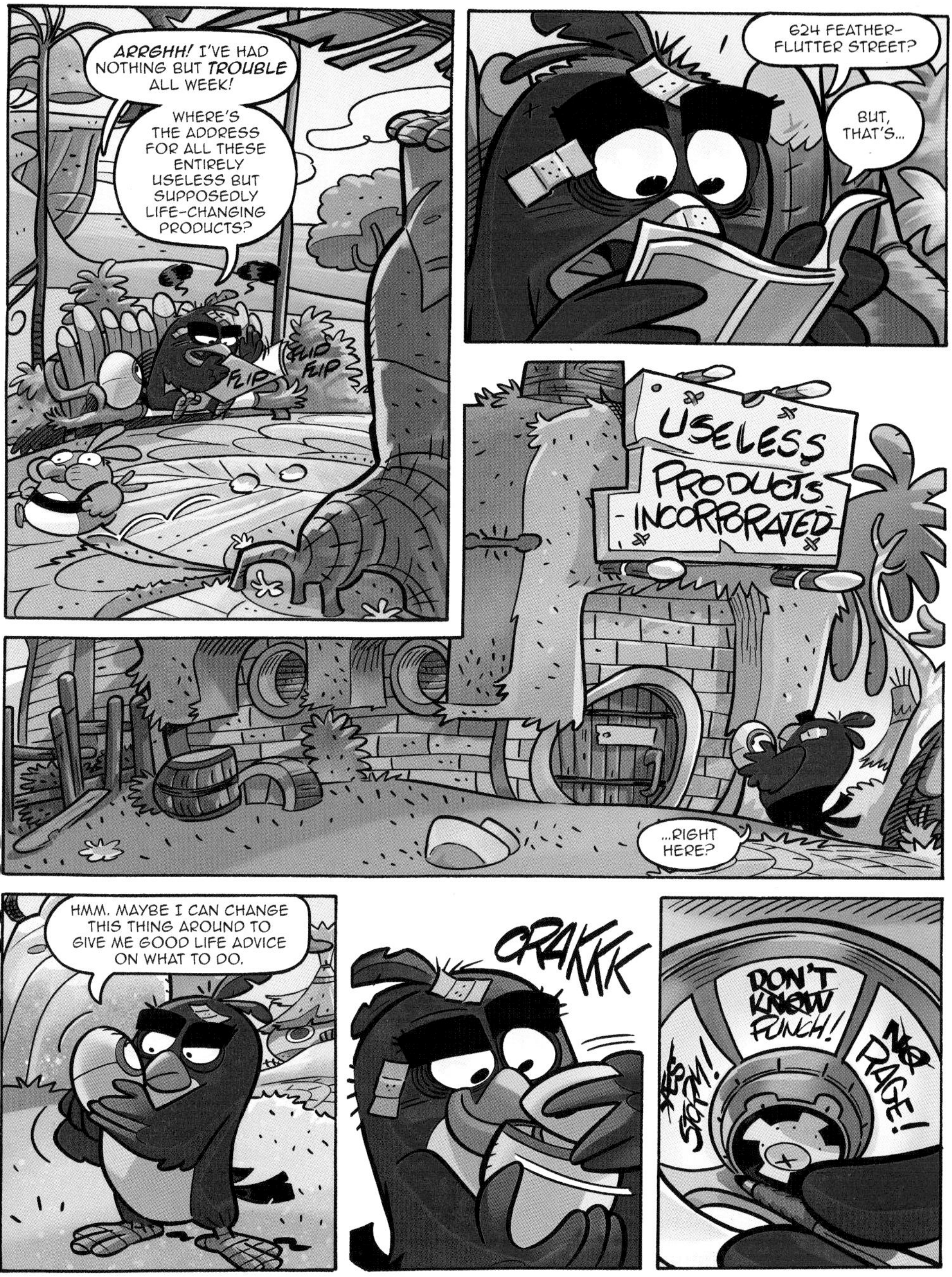

ARRGHH! I'VE HAD NOTHING BUT TROUBLE ALL WEEK!
WHERE'S THE ADDRESS FOR ALL THESE ENTIRELY USELESS BUT SUPPOSEDLY LIFE-CHANGING PRODUCTS?
FLIP FLIP FLIP
624 FEATHER-FLUTTER STREET?
BUT, THAT'S...
USELESS PRODUCTS INCORPORATED
...RIGHT HERE?
HMM. MAYBE I CAN CHANGE THIS THING AROUND TO GIVE ME GOOD LIFE ADVICE ON WHAT TO DO.
CRAKKK
DON'T KNOW PUNCH!
NO RAGE!
YES STOMP!

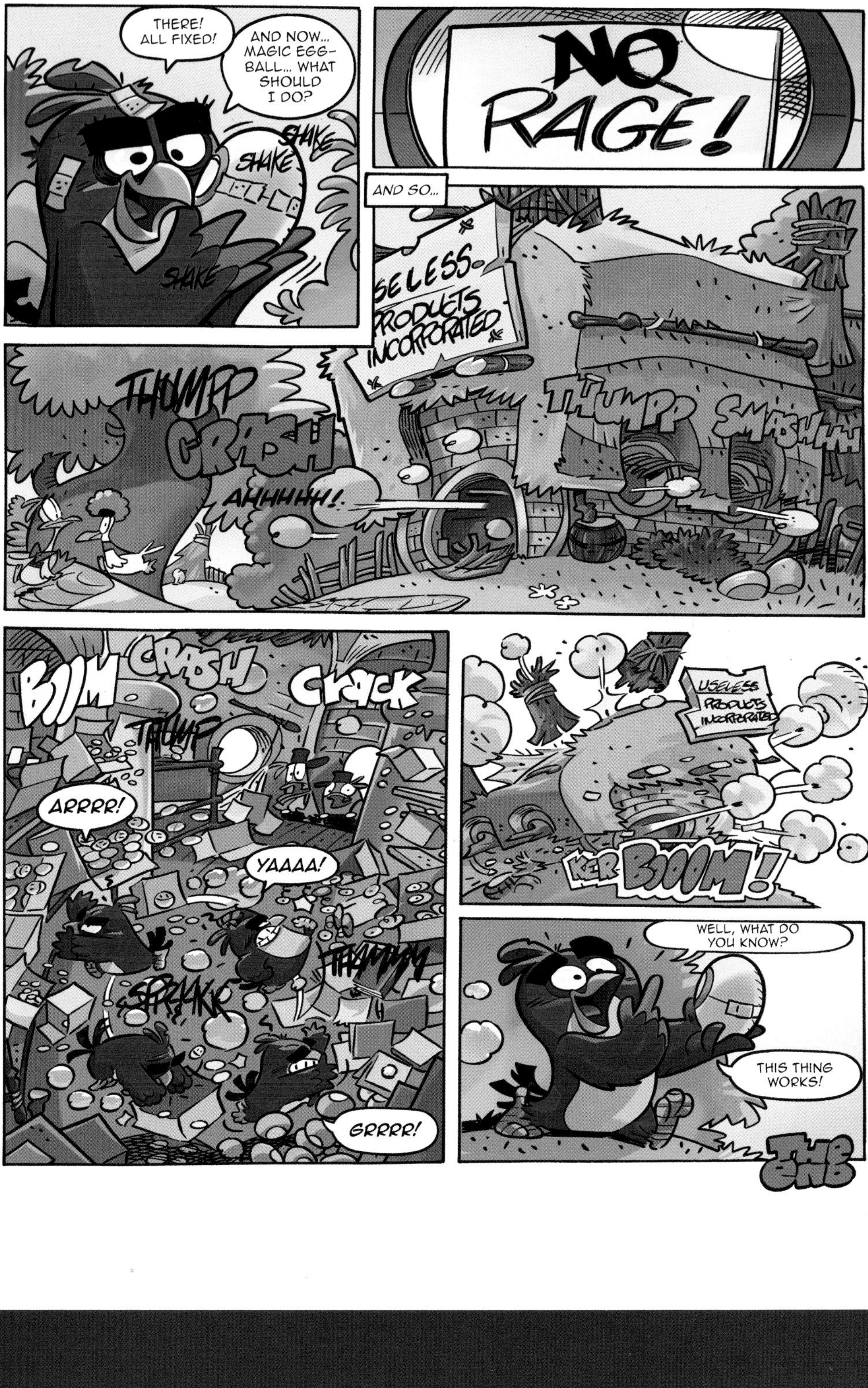
THERE! ALL FIXED!
AND NOW... MAGIC EGG-BALL... WHAT SHOULD I DO?
SHAKE
SHAKE
SHAKE
NO
RAGE!
AND SO...
USELESS PRODUCTS INCORPORATED
THUMPP
CRASH
AHHHHH!
THUMPP
SMASHHH
BOOM
CRASH
CRACK
THUMP
ARRRR!
YAAAA!
GRRRR!
USELESS PRODUCTS INCORPORATED
KER BOOOM!
WELL, WHAT DO YOU KNOW?
THIS THING WORKS!
THE END

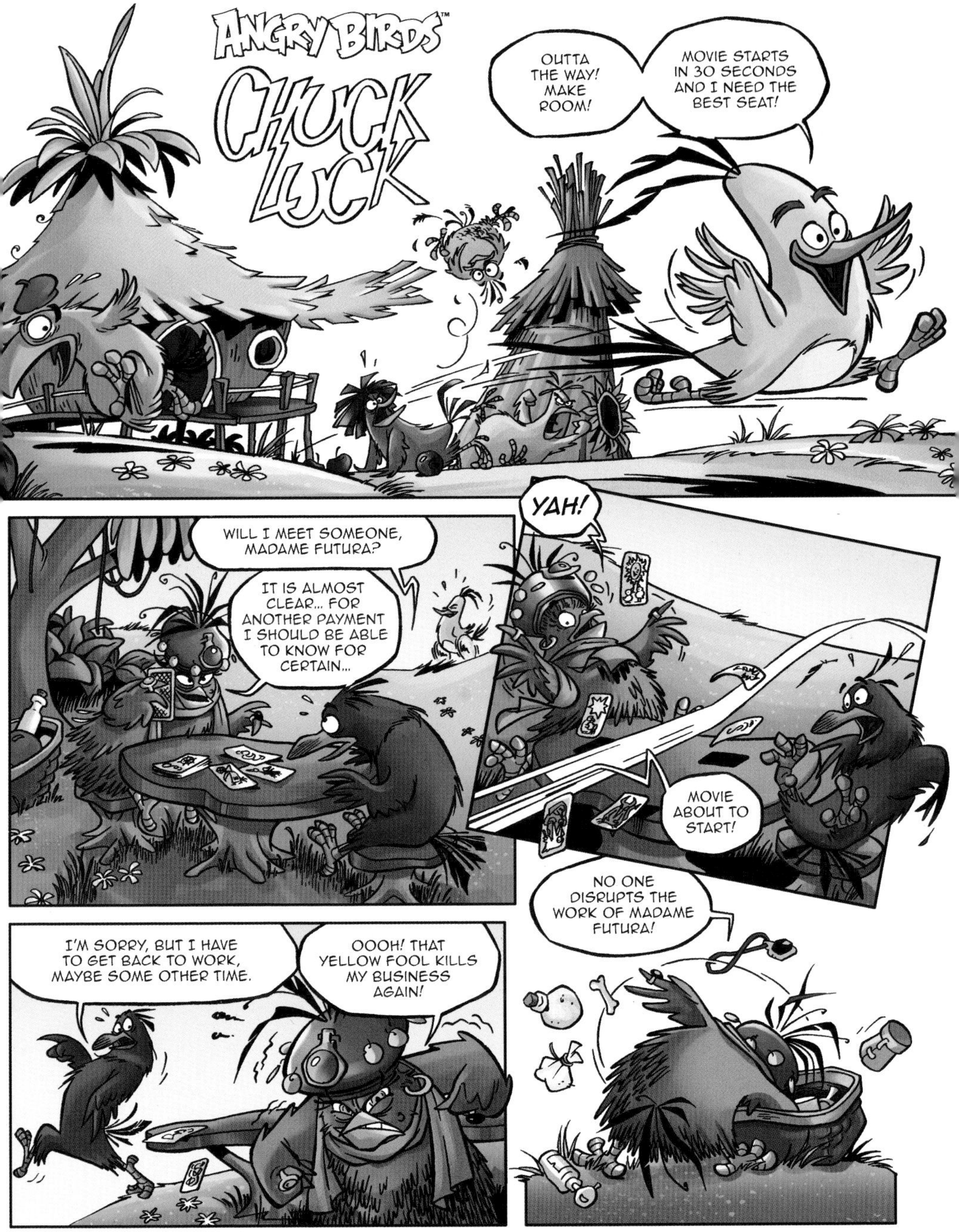
ANGRY BIRDS™
CHUCK LUCK
OUTTA THE WAY! MAKE ROOM!
MOVIE STARTS IN 30 SECONDS AND I NEED THE BEST SEAT!
WILL I MEET SOMEONE, MADAME FUTURA?
IT IS ALMOST CLEAR... FOR ANOTHER PAYMENT I SHOULD BE ABLE TO KNOW FOR CERTAIN...
YAH!
MOVIE ABOUT TO START!
NO ONE DISRUPTS THE WORK OF MADAME FUTURA!
I'M SORRY, BUT I HAVE TO GET BACK TO WORK, MAYBE SOME OTHER TIME.
OOOH! THAT YELLOW FOOL KILLS MY BUSINESS AGAIN!

SCRIPT BY **JEFF PARKER** • ART & INKS BY **CÈSAR FERIOLI** • COLORS BY **DIGIKORE STUDIOS**

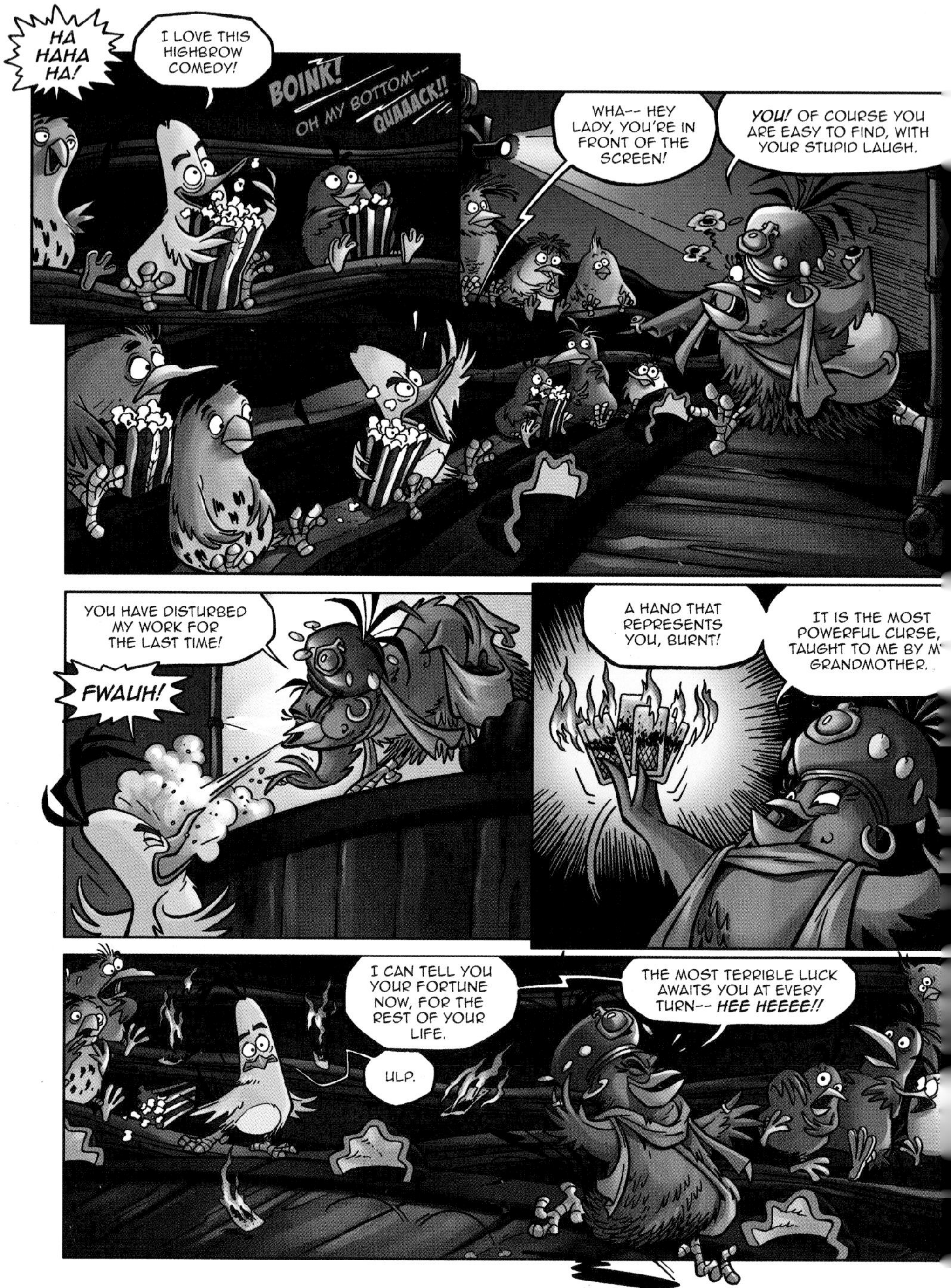
HA HAHA HA!
I LOVE THIS HIGHBROW COMEDY!
BOINK!
OH MY BOTTOM--
QUAAACK!!
WHA-- HEY LADY, YOU'RE IN FRONT OF THE SCREEN!
YOU! OF COURSE YOU ARE EASY TO FIND, WITH YOUR STUPID LAUGH.
YOU HAVE DISTURBED MY WORK FOR THE LAST TIME!
FWAUH!
A HAND THAT REPRESENTS YOU, BURNT!
IT IS THE MOST POWERFUL CURSE, TAUGHT TO ME BY M GRANDMOTHER.
I CAN TELL YOU YOUR FORTUNE NOW, FOR THE REST OF YOUR LIFE.
ULP.
THE MOST TERRIBLE LUCK AWAITS YOU AT EVERY TURN-- HEE HEEEE!!

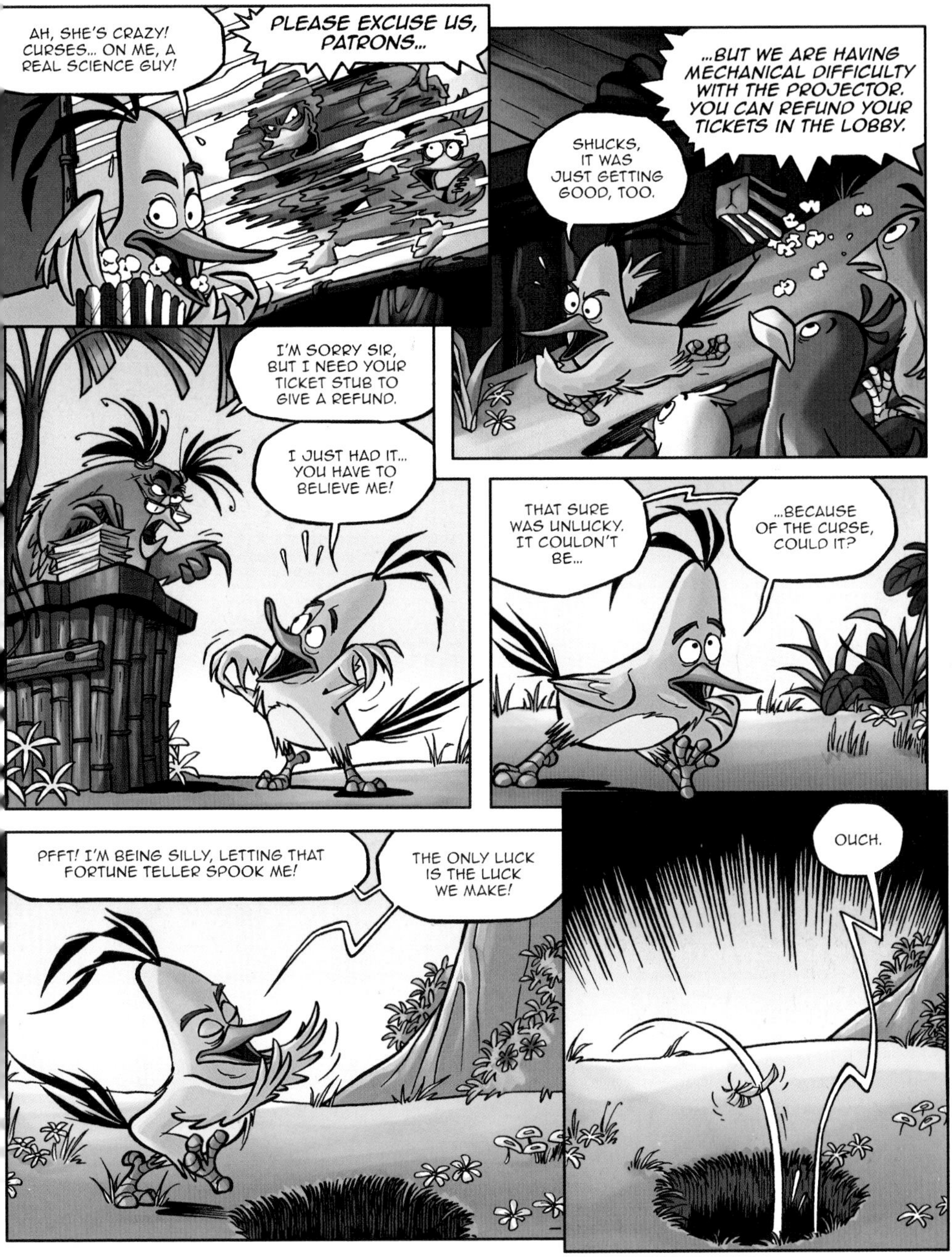
AH, SHE'S CRAZY! CURSES... ON ME, A REAL SCIENCE GUY!
PLEASE EXCUSE US, PATRONS...
...BUT WE ARE HAVING MECHANICAL DIFFICULTY WITH THE PROJECTOR. YOU CAN REFUND YOUR TICKETS IN THE LOBBY.
SHUCKS, IT WAS JUST GETTING GOOD, TOO.
I'M SORRY SIR, BUT I NEED YOUR TICKET STUB TO GIVE A REFUND.
I JUST HAD IT... YOU HAVE TO BELIEVE ME!
THAT SURE WAS UNLUCKY. IT COULDN'T BE...
...BECAUSE OF THE CURSE, COULD IT?
PFFT! I'M BEING SILLY, LETTING THAT FORTUNE TELLER SPOOK ME!
THE ONLY LUCK IS THE LUCK WE MAKE!
OUCH.

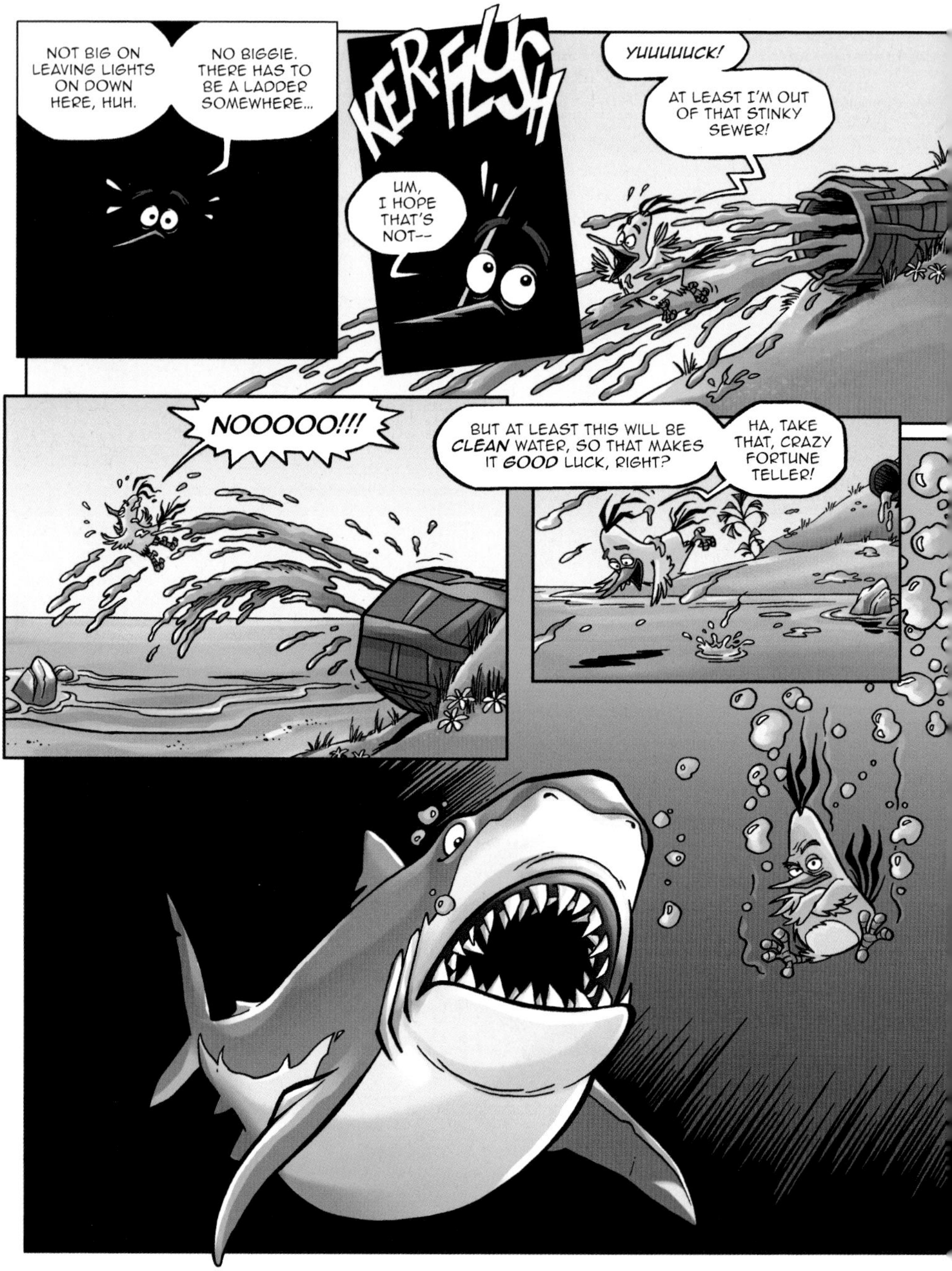
NOT BIG ON LEAVING LIGHTS ON DOWN HERE, HUH.
NO BIGGIE. THERE HAS TO BE A LADDER SOMEWHERE...
KER-FLUSH
UM, I HOPE THAT'S NOT--
YUUUUUCK!
AT LEAST I'M OUT OF THAT STINKY SEWER!
NOOOOO!!!
BUT AT LEAST THIS WILL BE CLEAN WATER, SO THAT MAKES IT GOOD LUCK, RIGHT?
HA, TAKE THAT, CRAZY FORTUNE TELLER!

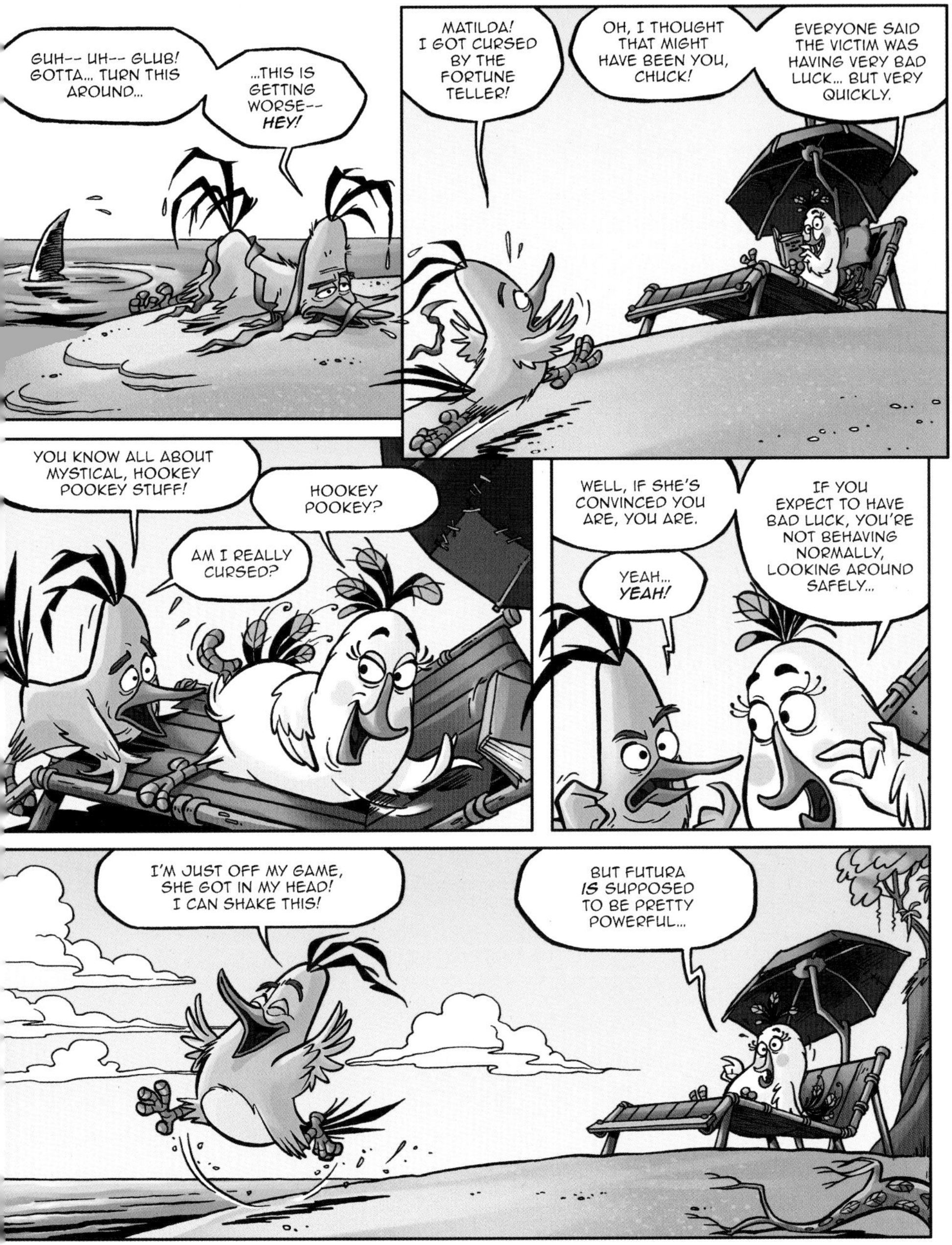
GUH-- UH-- GLUB! GOTTA... TURN THIS AROUND...
...THIS IS GETTING WORSE-- HEY!
MATILDA! I GOT CURSED BY THE FORTUNE TELLER!
OH, I THOUGHT THAT MIGHT HAVE BEEN YOU, CHUCK!
EVERYONE SAID THE VICTIM WAS HAVING VERY BAD LUCK... BUT VERY QUICKLY.
YOU KNOW ALL ABOUT MYSTICAL, HOOKEY POOKEY STUFF!
HOOKEY POOKEY?
AM I REALLY CURSED?
WELL, IF SHE'S CONVINCED YOU ARE, YOU ARE.
IF YOU EXPECT TO HAVE BAD LUCK, YOU'RE NOT BEHAVING NORMALLY, LOOKING AROUND SAFELY...
YEAH... YEAH!
I'M JUST OFF MY GAME, SHE GOT IN MY HEAD! I CAN SHAKE THIS!
BUT FUTURA IS SUPPOSED TO BE PRETTY POWERFUL...

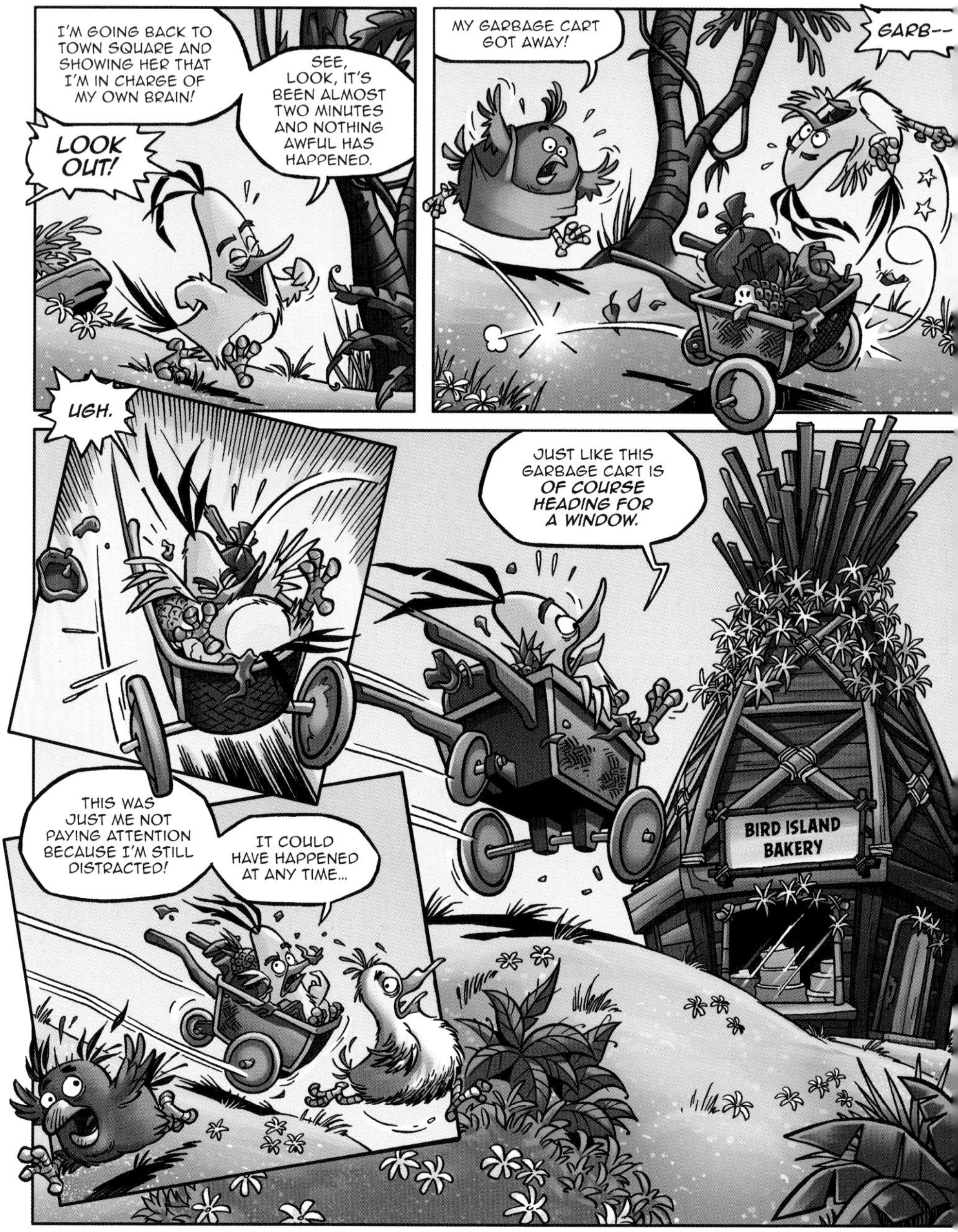
I'M GOING BACK TO TOWN SQUARE AND SHOWING HER THAT I'M IN CHARGE OF MY OWN BRAIN!
SEE, LOOK, IT'S BEEN ALMOST TWO MINUTES AND NOTHING AWFUL HAS HAPPENED.
LOOK OUT!
MY GARBAGE CART GOT AWAY!
GARB--
UGH.
JUST LIKE THIS GARBAGE CART IS OF COURSE HEADING FOR A WINDOW.
BIRD ISLAND BAKERY
THIS WAS JUST ME NOT PAYING ATTENTION BECAUSE I'M STILL DISTRACTED!
IT COULD HAVE HAPPENED AT ANY TIME...

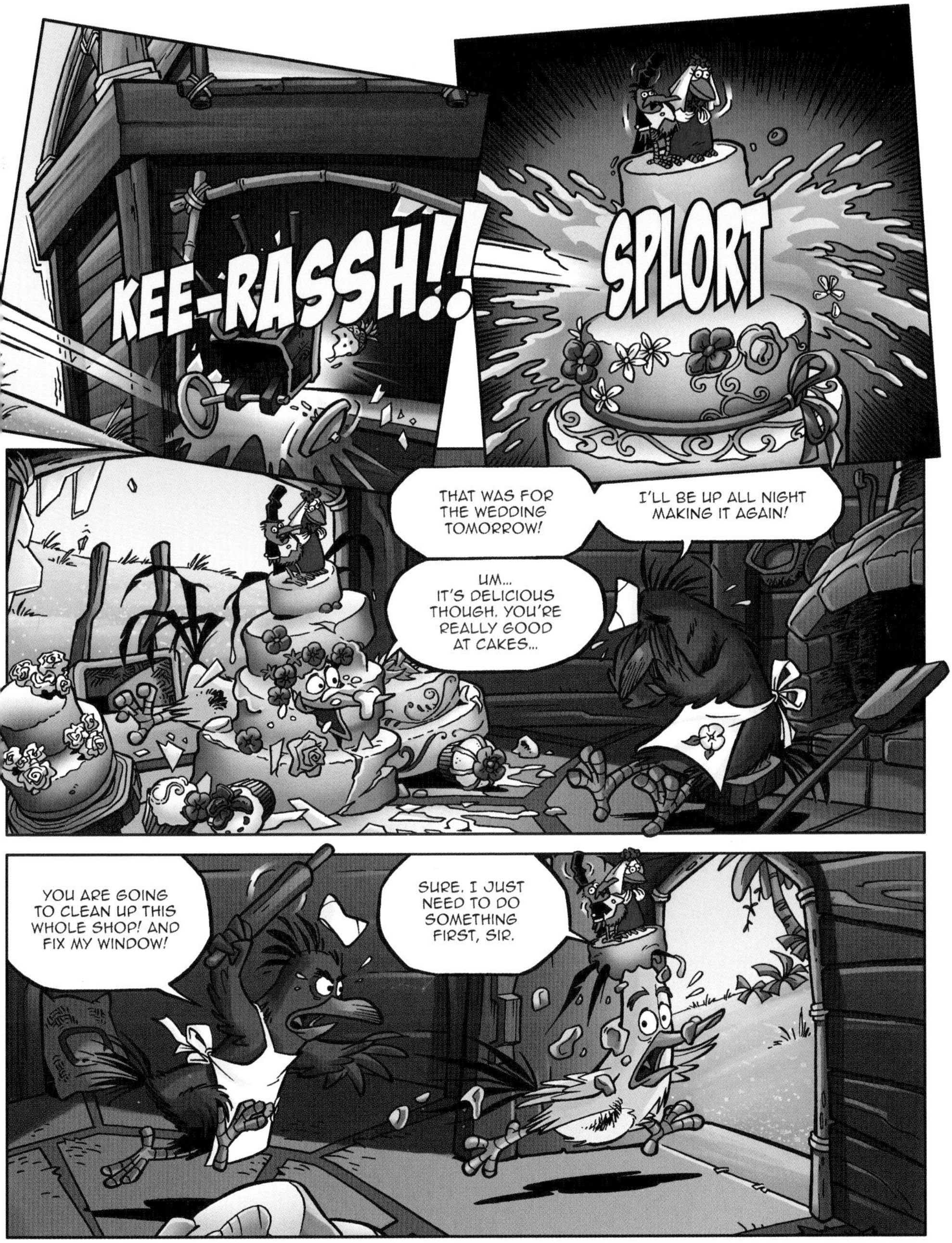
KEE-RASSH!!
SPLORT
THAT WAS FOR THE WEDDING TOMORROW!
I'LL BE UP ALL NIGHT MAKING IT AGAIN!
UM... IT'S DELICIOUS THOUGH. YOU'RE REALLY GOOD AT CAKES...
YOU ARE GOING TO CLEAN UP THIS WHOLE SHOP! AND FIX MY WINDOW!
SURE. I JUST NEED TO DO SOMETHING FIRST, SIR.

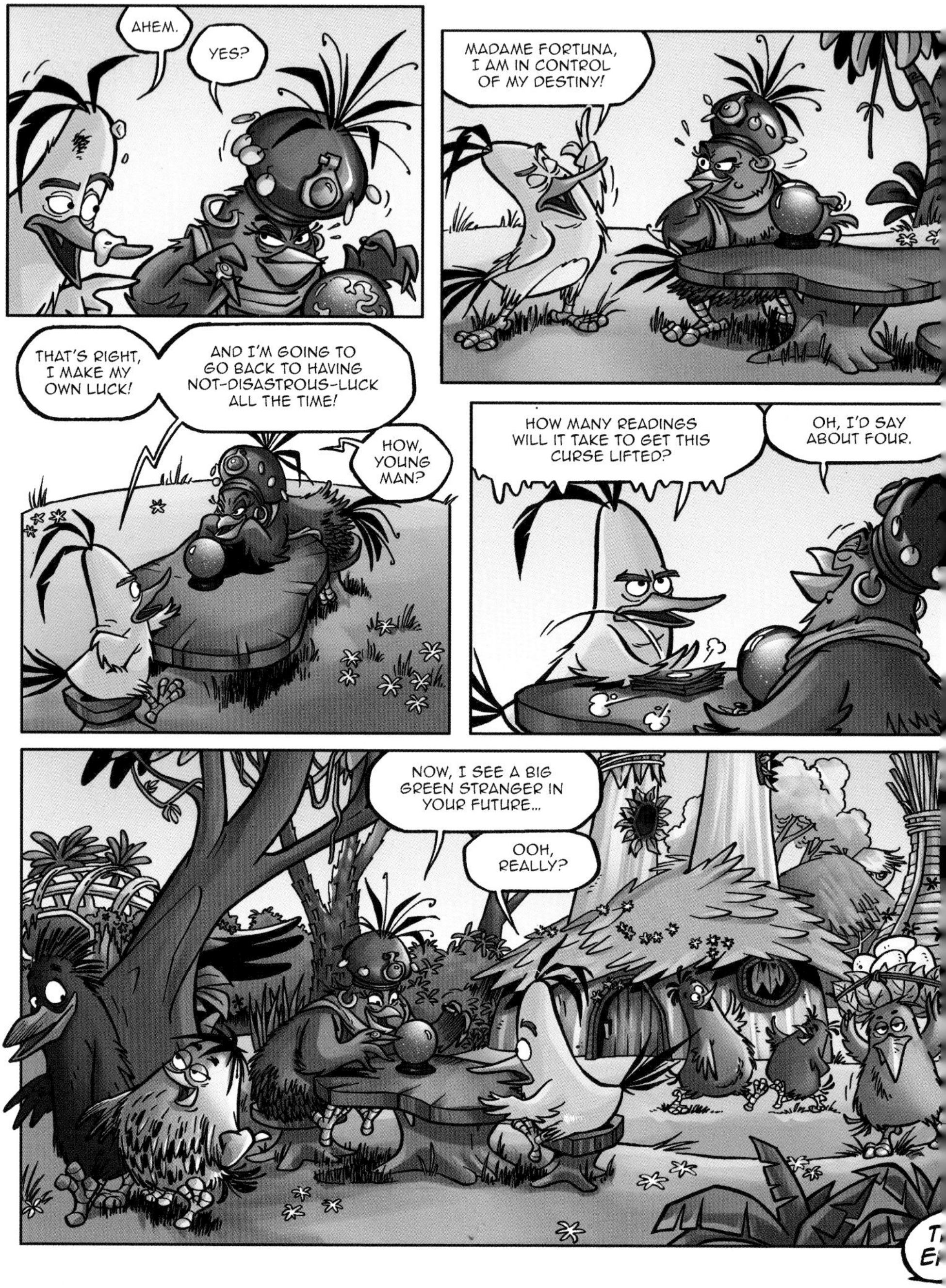
AHEM.
YES?
MADAME FORTUNA, I AM IN CONTROL OF MY DESTINY!
THAT'S RIGHT, I MAKE MY OWN LUCK!
AND I'M GOING TO GO BACK TO HAVING NOT-DISASTROUS-LUCK ALL THE TIME!
HOW, YOUNG MAN?
HOW MANY READINGS WILL IT TAKE TO GET THIS CURSE LIFTED?
OH, I'D SAY ABOUT FOUR.
NOW, I SEE A BIG GREEN STRANGER IN YOUR FUTURE...
OOH, REALLY?

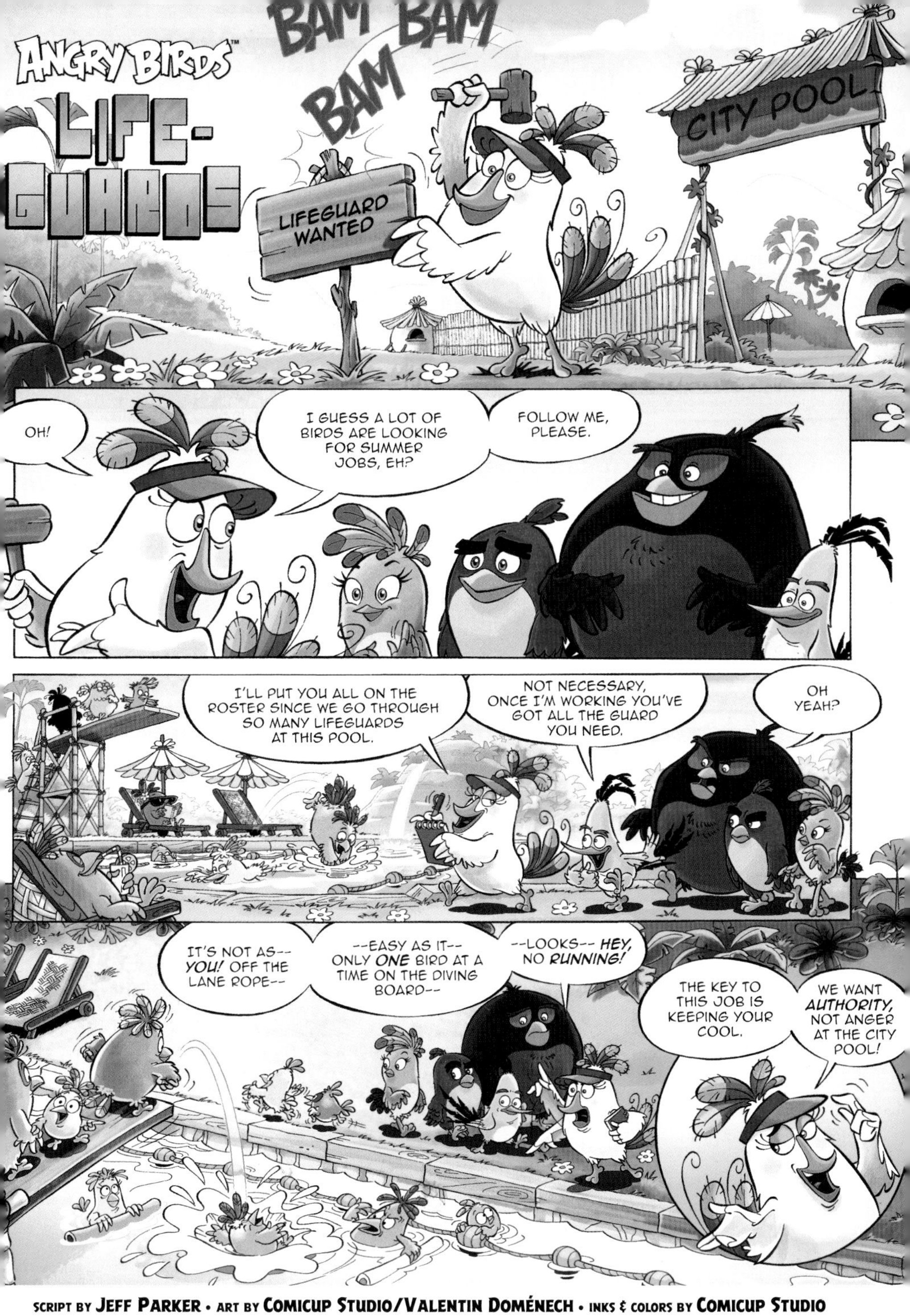
ANGRY BIRDS™
LIFE-GUARDS
BAM BAM
BAM
LIFEGUARD WANTED
CITY POOL
OH!
I GUESS A LOT OF BIRDS ARE LOOKING FOR SUMMER JOBS, EH?
FOLLOW ME, PLEASE.
I'LL PUT YOU ALL ON THE ROSTER SINCE WE GO THROUGH SO MANY LIFEGUARDS AT THIS POOL.
NOT NECESSARY, ONCE I'M WORKING YOU'VE GOT ALL THE GUARD YOU NEED.
OH YEAH?
IT'S NOT AS-- *YOU!* OFF THE LANE ROPE--
--EASY AS IT-- ONLY *ONE* BIRD AT A TIME ON THE DIVING BOARD--
--LOOKS-- *HEY, NO RUNNING!*
THE KEY TO THIS JOB IS KEEPING YOUR COOL.
WE WANT *AUTHORITY,* NOT ANGER AT THE CITY POOL!

SCRIPT BY **JEFF PARKER** • ART BY **COMICUP STUDIO/VALENTIN DOMÉNECH** • INKS & COLORS BY **COMICUP STUDIO**

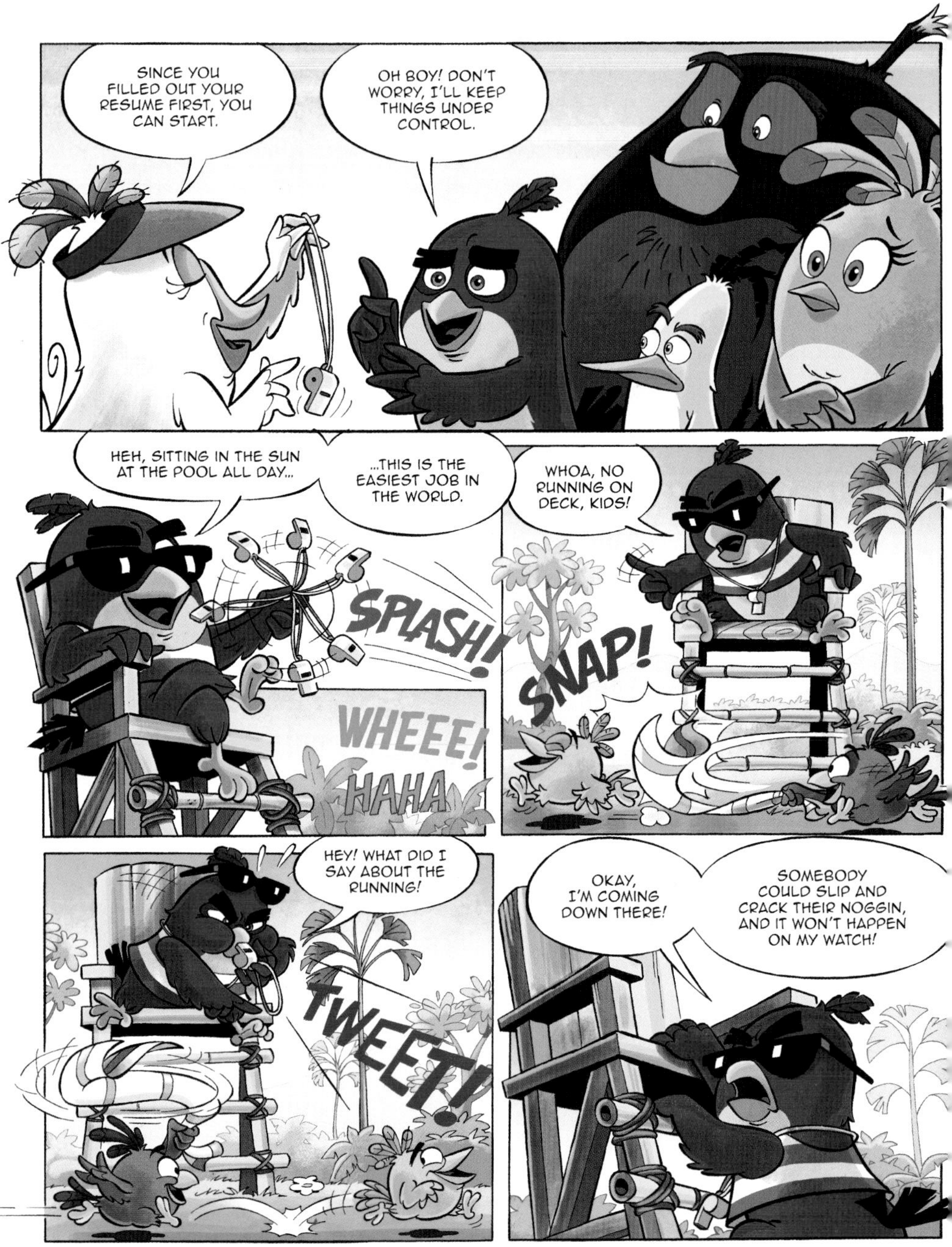
SINCE YOU FILLED OUT YOUR RESUME FIRST, YOU CAN START.
OH BOY! DON'T WORRY, I'LL KEEP THINGS UNDER CONTROL.
HEH, SITTING IN THE SUN AT THE POOL ALL DAY...
...THIS IS THE EASIEST JOB IN THE WORLD.
SPLASH!
WHEEE!
HAHA
WHOA, NO RUNNING ON DECK, KIDS!
SNAP!
HEY! WHAT DID I SAY ABOUT THE RUNNING!
TWEET!
OKAY, I'M COMING DOWN THERE!
SOMEBODY COULD SLIP AND CRACK THEIR NOGGIN, AND IT WON'T HAPPEN ON MY WATCH!

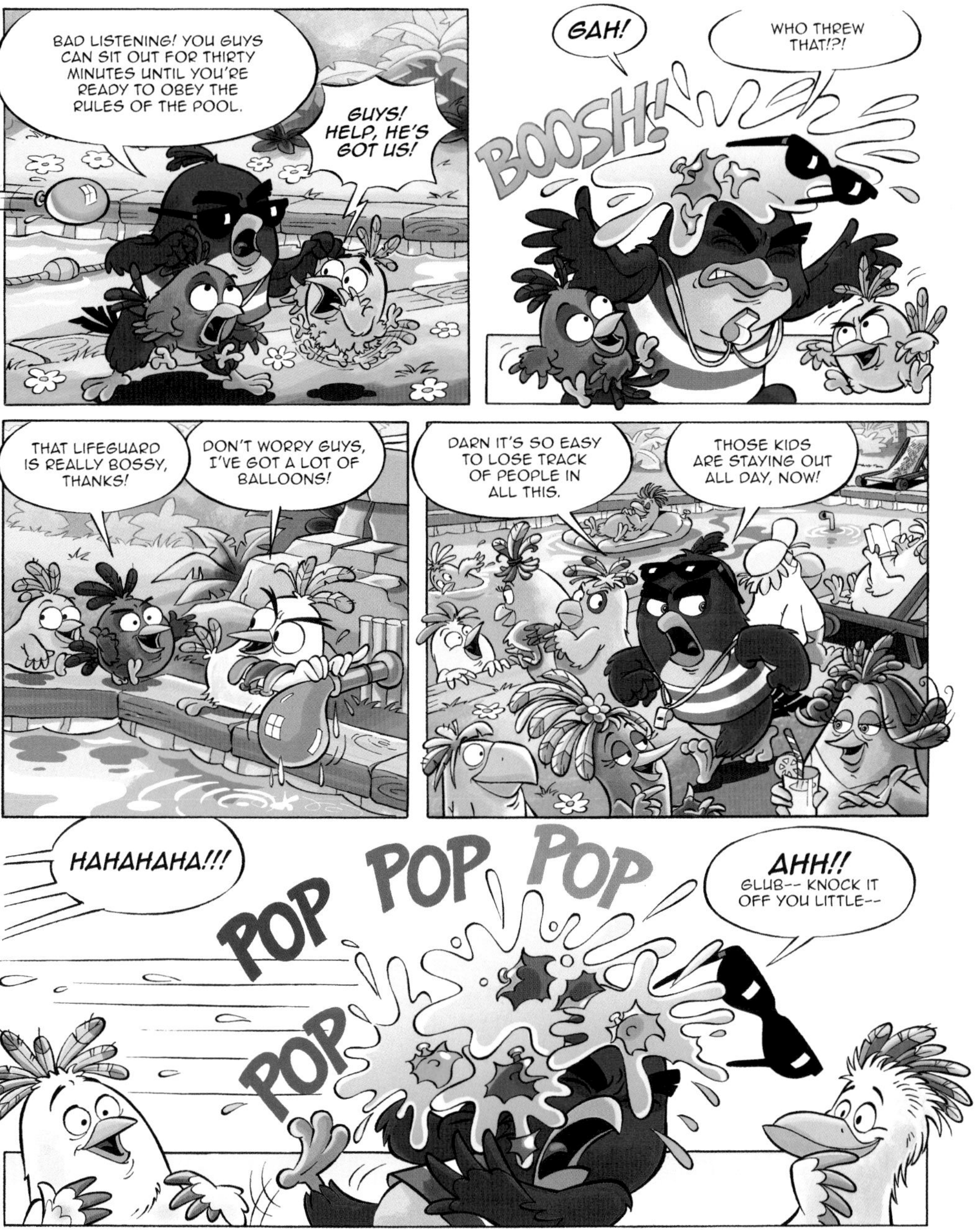
BAD LISTENING! YOU GUYS CAN SIT OUT FOR THIRTY MINUTES UNTIL YOU'RE READY TO OBEY THE RULES OF THE POOL.
GUYS! HELP, HE'S GOT US!
GAH!
WHO THREW THAT!?!
BOOSH!
THAT LIFEGUARD IS REALLY BOSSY, THANKS!
DON'T WORRY GUYS, I'VE GOT A LOT OF BALLOONS!
DARN IT'S SO EASY TO LOSE TRACK OF PEOPLE IN ALL THIS.
THOSE KIDS ARE STAYING OUT ALL DAY, NOW!
HAHAHAHA!!!
POP POP POP POP
POP
AHH!! GLUB-- KNOCK IT OFF YOU LITTLE--

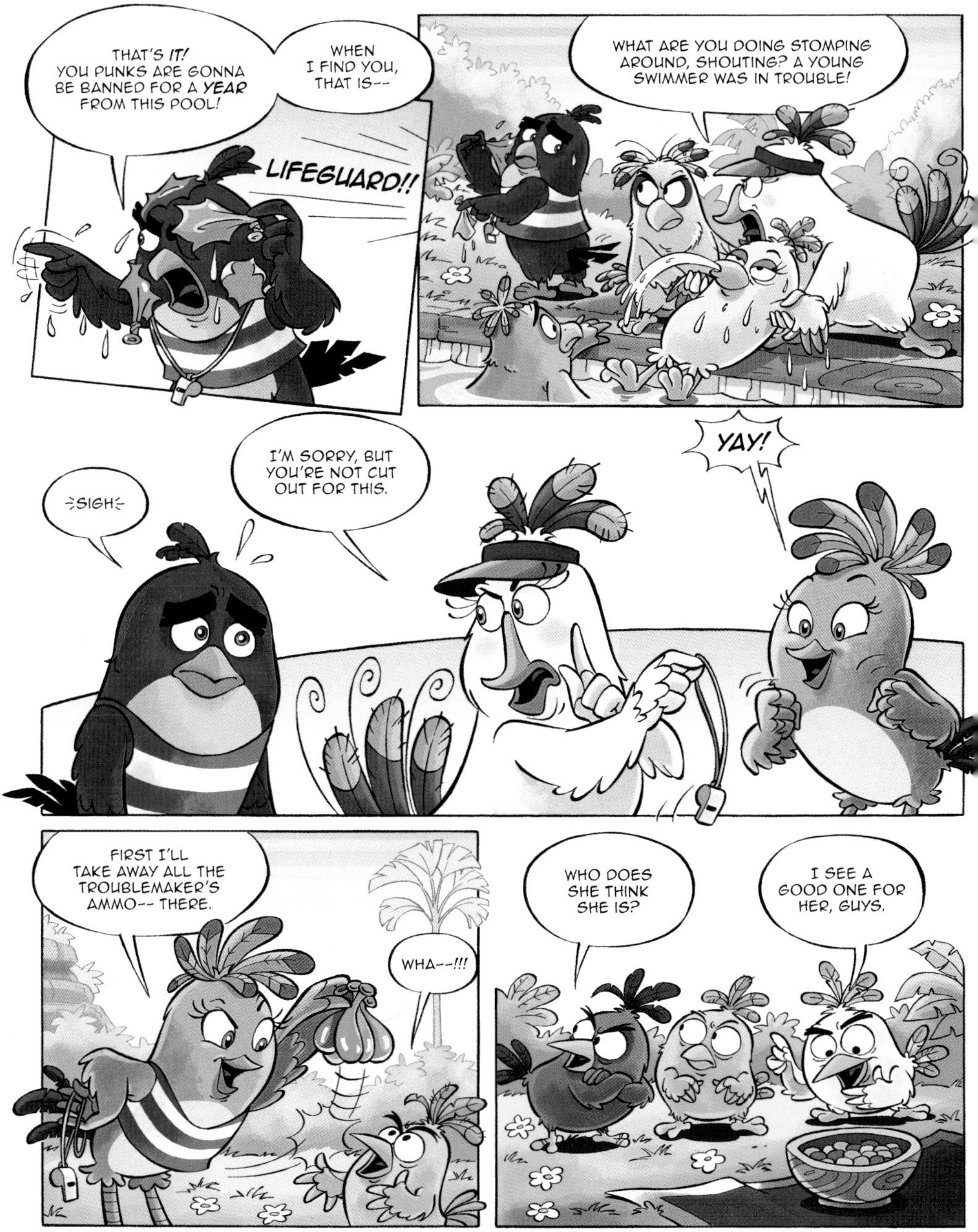
THAT'S IT! YOU PUNKS ARE GONNA BE BANNED FOR A YEAR FROM THIS POOL!
WHEN I FIND YOU, THAT IS--
LIFEGUARD!!
WHAT ARE YOU DOING STOMPING AROUND, SHOUTING? A YOUNG SWIMMER WAS IN TROUBLE!
-SIGH-
I'M SORRY, BUT YOU'RE NOT CUT OUT FOR THIS.
YAY!
FIRST I'LL TAKE AWAY ALL THE TROUBLEMAKER'S AMMO-- THERE.
WHA--!!!
WHO DOES SHE THINK SHE IS?
I SEE A GOOD ONE FOR HER, GUYS.

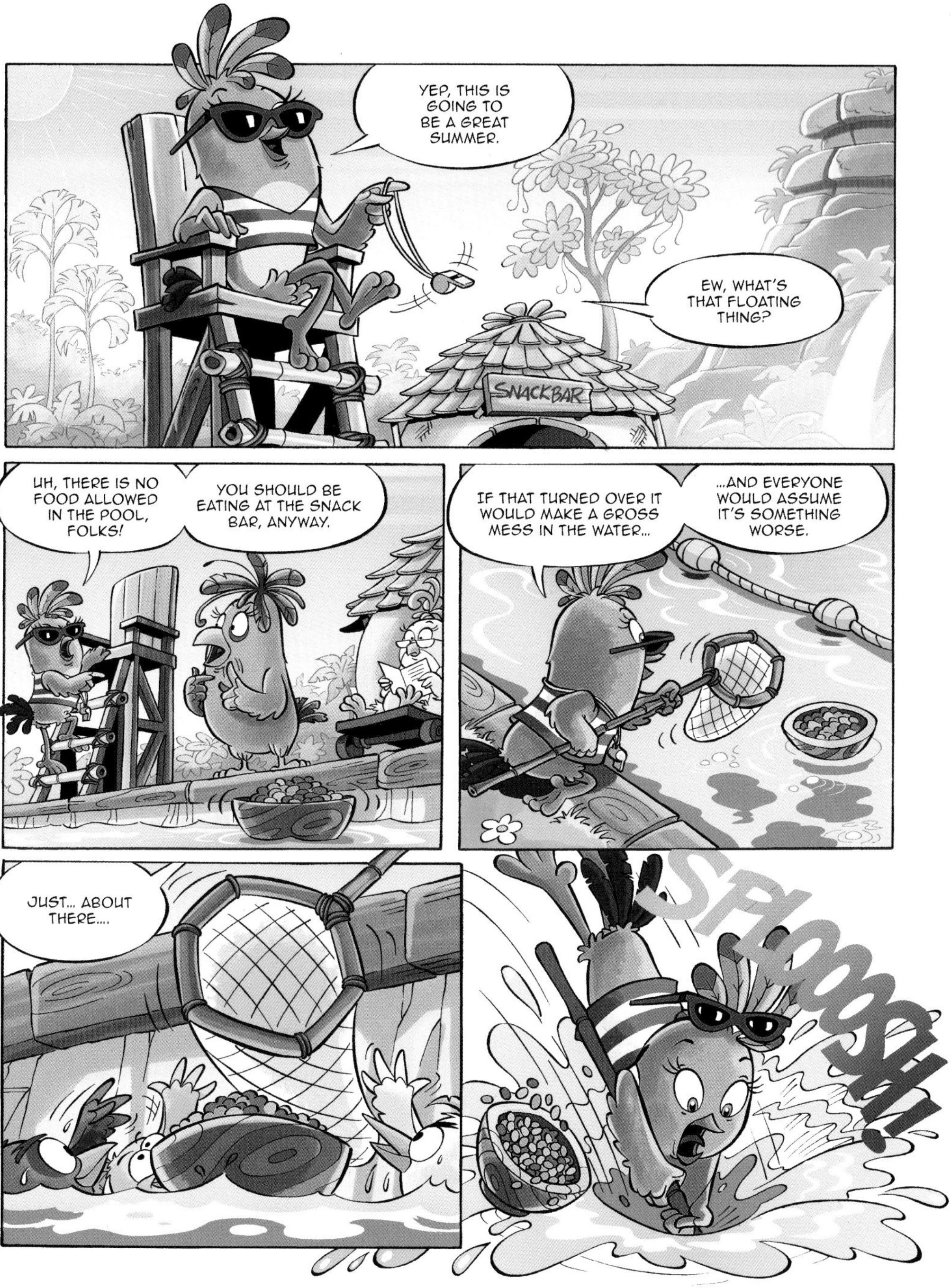
YEP, THIS IS GOING TO BE A GREAT SUMMER.
EW, WHAT'S THAT FLOATING THING?
SNACKBAR
UH, THERE IS NO FOOD ALLOWED IN THE POOL, FOLKS!
YOU SHOULD BE EATING AT THE SNACK BAR, ANYWAY.
IF THAT TURNED OVER IT WOULD MAKE A GROSS MESS IN THE WATER...
...AND EVERYONE WOULD ASSUME IT'S SOMETHING WORSE.
JUST... ABOUT THERE....
SPLOOSH!

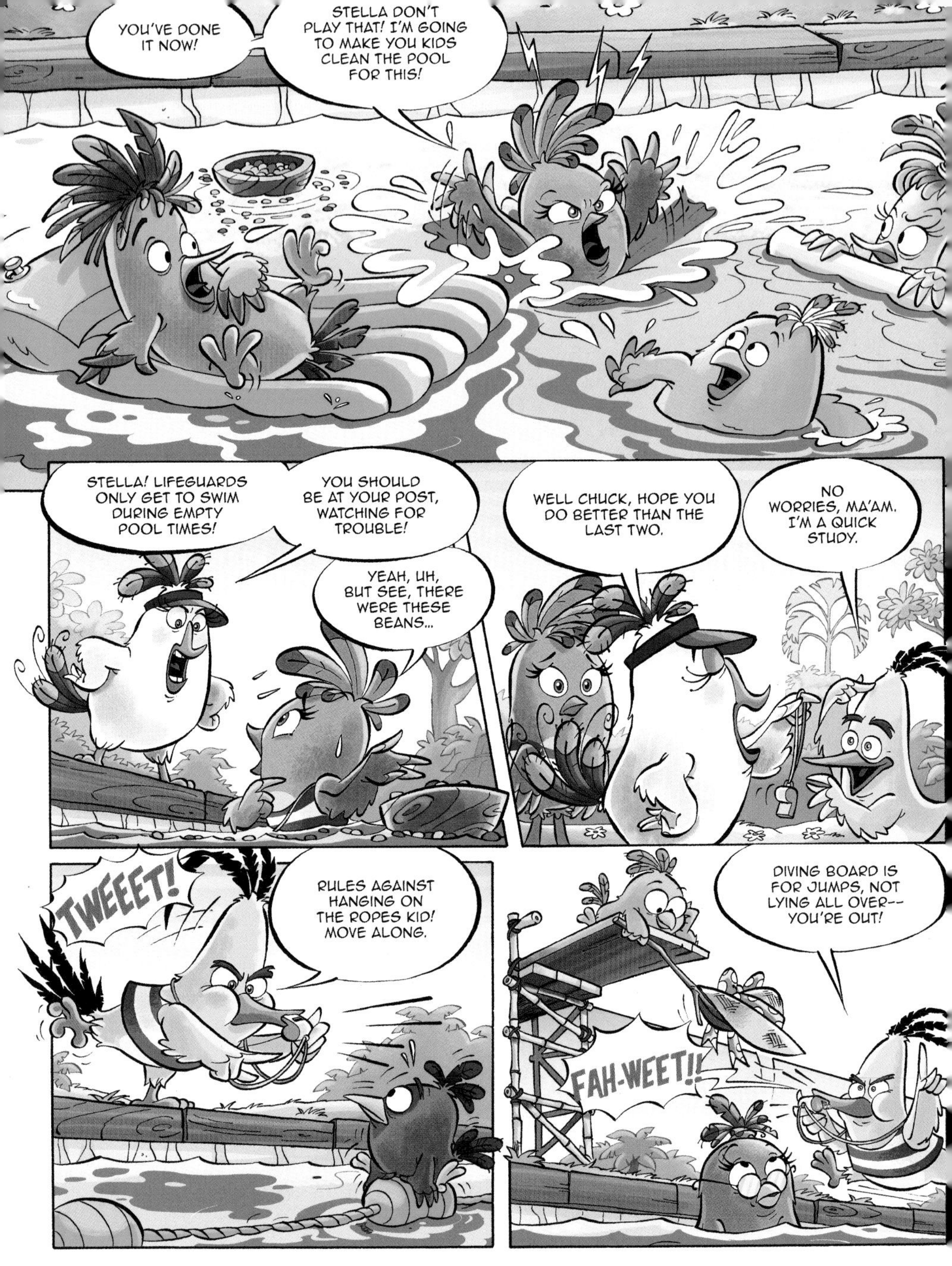

YOU'VE DONE IT NOW!
STELLA DON'T PLAY THAT! I'M GOING TO MAKE YOU KIDS CLEAN THE POOL FOR THIS!
STELLA! LIFEGUARDS ONLY GET TO SWIM DURING EMPTY POOL TIMES!
YOU SHOULD BE AT YOUR POST, WATCHING FOR TROUBLE!
YEAH, UH, BUT SEE, THERE WERE THESE BEANS...
WELL CHUCK, HOPE YOU DO BETTER THAN THE LAST TWO.
NO WORRIES, MA'AM. I'M A QUICK STUDY.
TWEEET!
RULES AGAINST HANGING ON THE ROPES KID! MOVE ALONG.
DIVING BOARD IS FOR JUMPS, NOT LYING ALL OVER-- YOU'RE OUT!
FAH-WEET!!

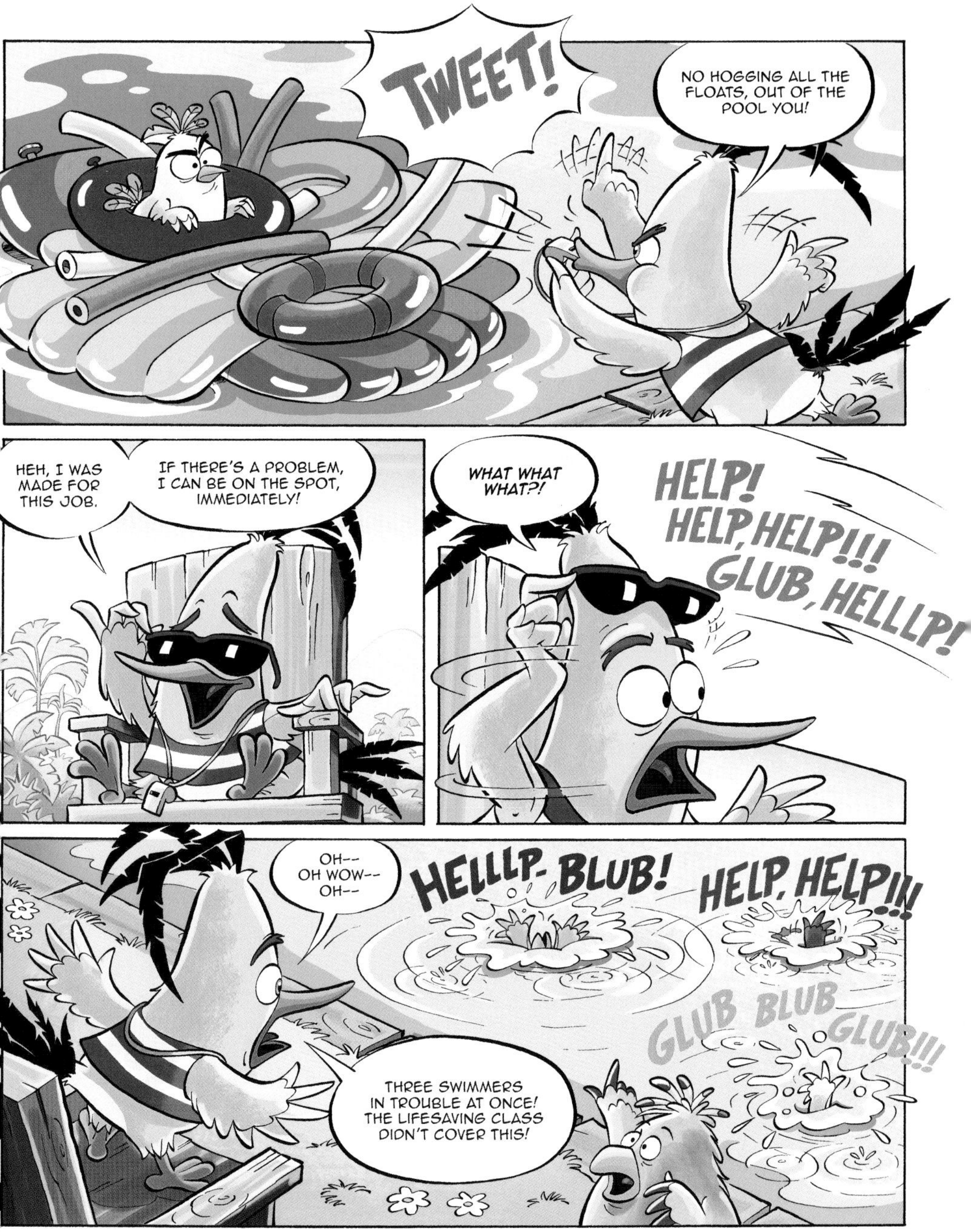
TWEET!
NO HOGGING ALL THE FLOATS, OUT OF THE POOL YOU!
HEH, I WAS MADE FOR THIS JOB.
IF THERE'S A PROBLEM, I CAN BE ON THE SPOT, IMMEDIATELY!
WHAT WHAT WHAT?!
HELP! HELP, HELP!!! GLUB, HELLLP!
OH-- OH WOW-- OH--
HELLLP- BLUB!
HELP, HELP!!!
GLUB BLUB GLUB!!!
THREE SWIMMERS IN TROUBLE AT ONCE! THE LIFESAVING CLASS DIDN'T COVER THIS!

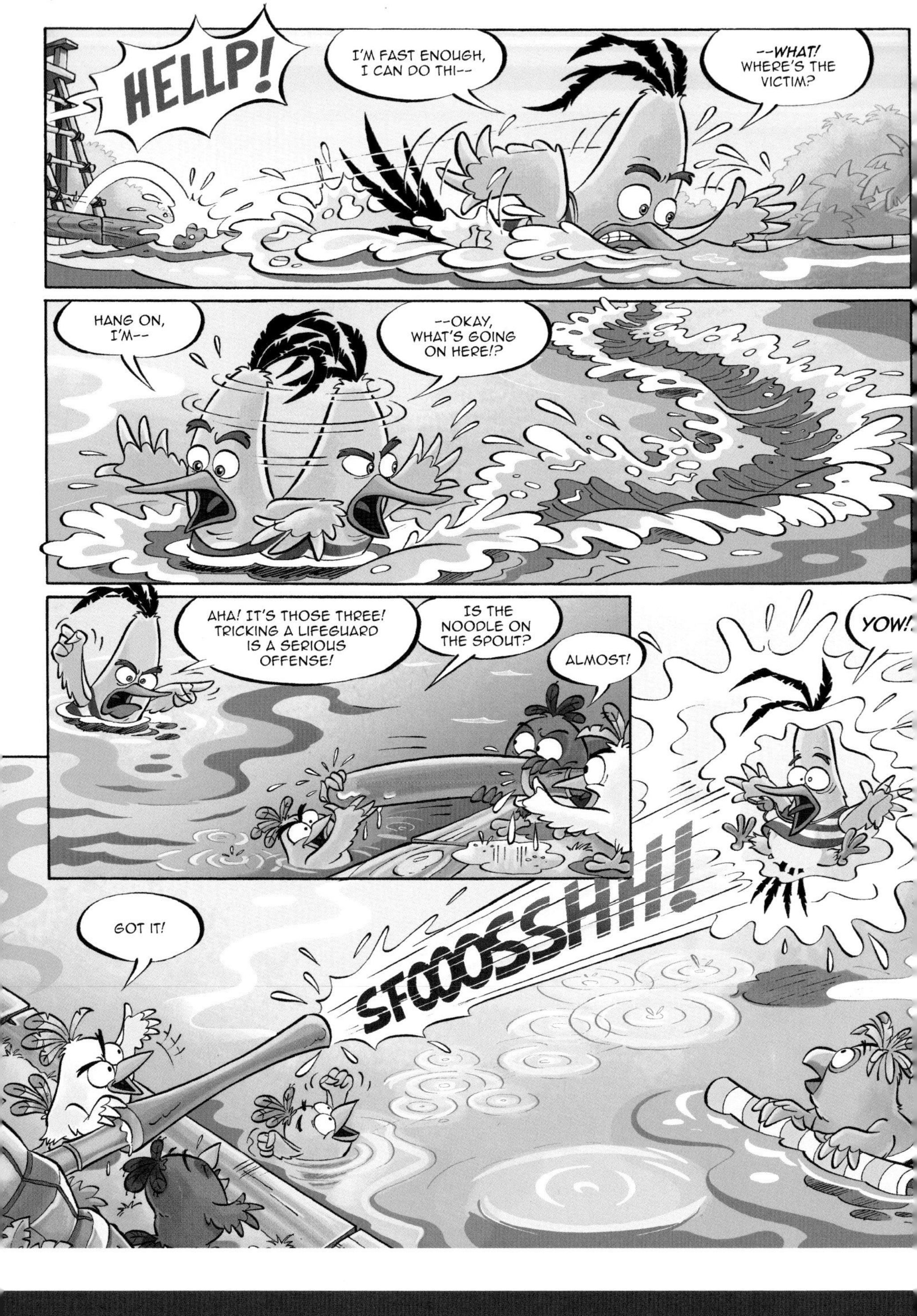
HELLP!
I'M FAST ENOUGH, I CAN DO THI--
--WHAT! WHERE'S THE VICTIM?
HANG ON, I'M--
--OKAY, WHAT'S GOING ON HERE!?
AHA! IT'S THOSE THREE! TRICKING A LIFEGUARD IS A SERIOUS OFFENSE!
IS THE NOODLE ON THE SPOUT?
ALMOST!
YOW!
GOT IT!
SFOOOSSHH!!

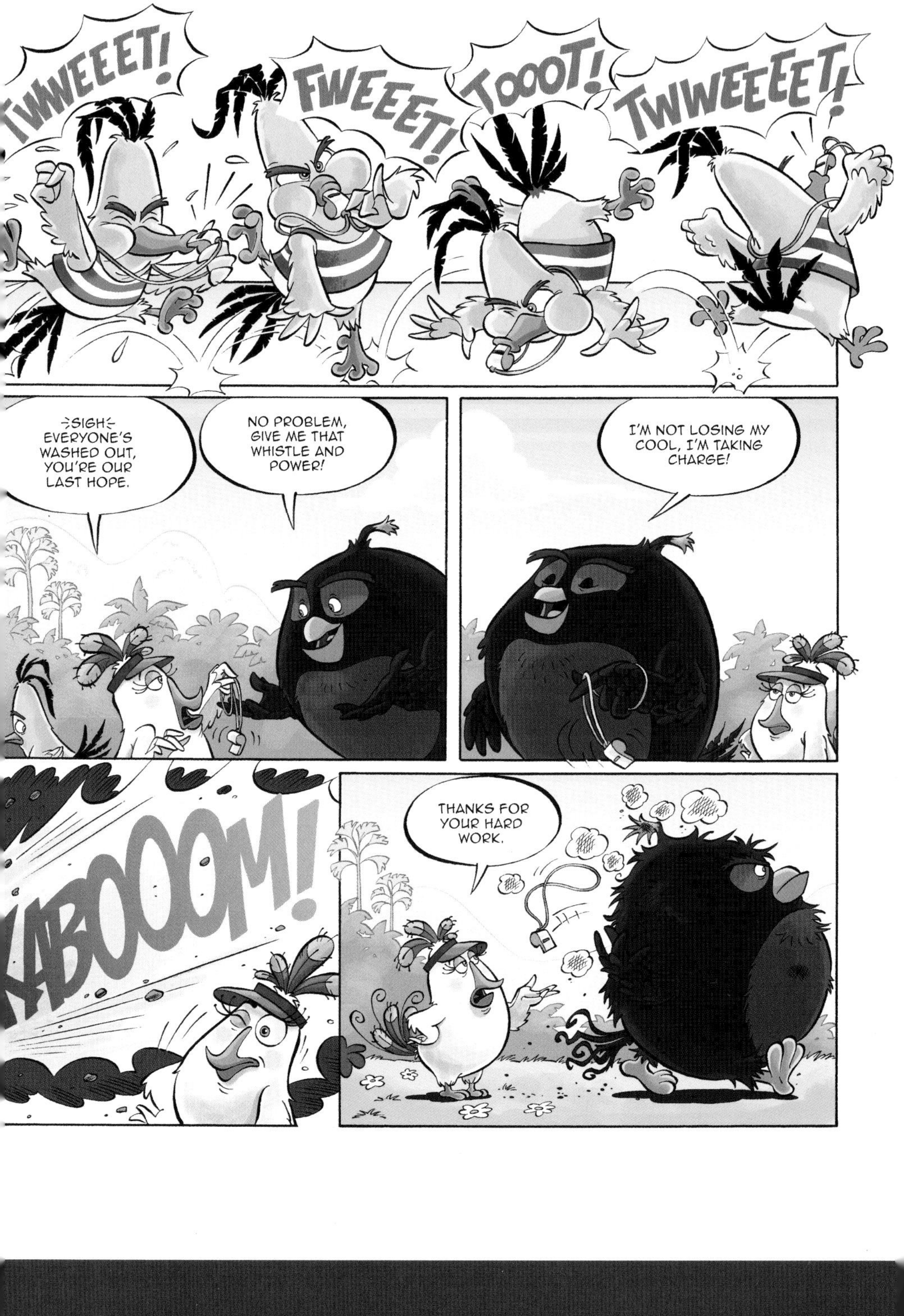
TWWEEET!
FWEEET!
TOOOT!
TWWEEEET!
-SIGH- EVERYONE'S WASHED OUT, YOU'RE OUR LAST HOPE.
NO PROBLEM, GIVE ME THAT WHISTLE AND POWER!
I'M NOT LOSING MY COOL, I'M TAKING CHARGE!
KABOOOM!
THANKS FOR YOUR HARD WORK.

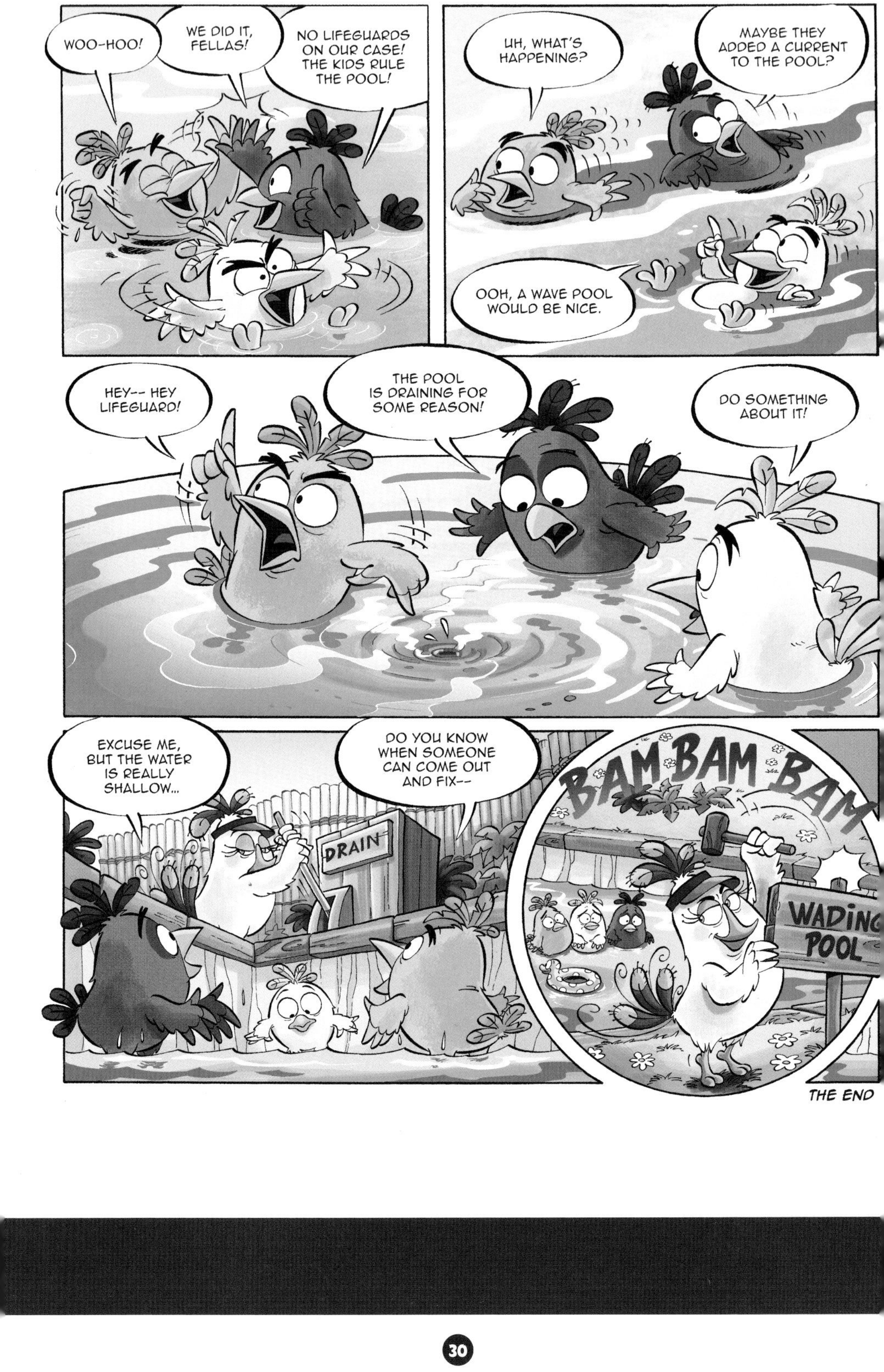
WOO-HOO!
WE DID IT, FELLAS!
NO LIFEGUARDS ON OUR CASE! THE KIDS RULE THE POOL!
UH, WHAT'S HAPPENING?
MAYBE THEY ADDED A CURRENT TO THE POOL?
OOH, A WAVE POOL WOULD BE NICE.
HEY-- HEY LIFEGUARD!
THE POOL IS DRAINING FOR SOME REASON!
DO SOMETHING ABOUT IT!
EXCUSE ME, BUT THE WATER IS REALLY SHALLOW...
DO YOU KNOW WHEN SOMEONE CAN COME OUT AND FIX--
DRAIN
BAM BAM BAM
WADING POOL
THE END

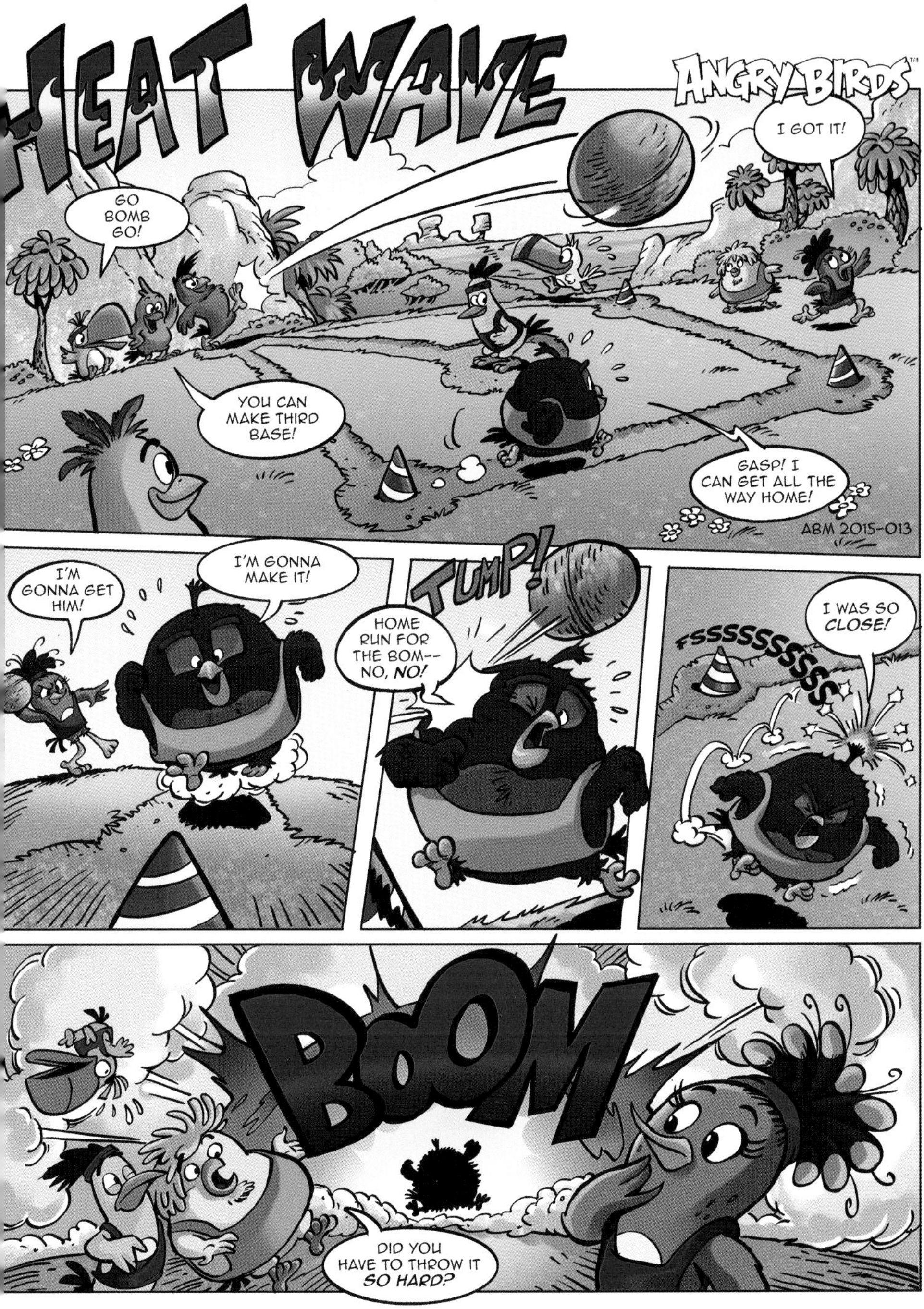
HEAT WAVE
ANGRY BIRDS
GO BOMB GO!
I GOT IT!
YOU CAN MAKE THIRD BASE!
GASP! I CAN GET ALL THE WAY HOME!
ABM 2015-013
I'M GONNA GET HIM!
I'M GONNA MAKE IT!
TUMP!
HOME RUN FOR THE BOM-- NO, NO!
FSSSSSSSSSSS
I WAS SO CLOSE!
BOOM
DID YOU HAVE TO THROW IT SO HARD?

SCRIPT BY **JEFF PARKER** • ART & INKS BY **THOMAS CABELLIC** • COLORS BY **DIGIKORE STUDIOS**

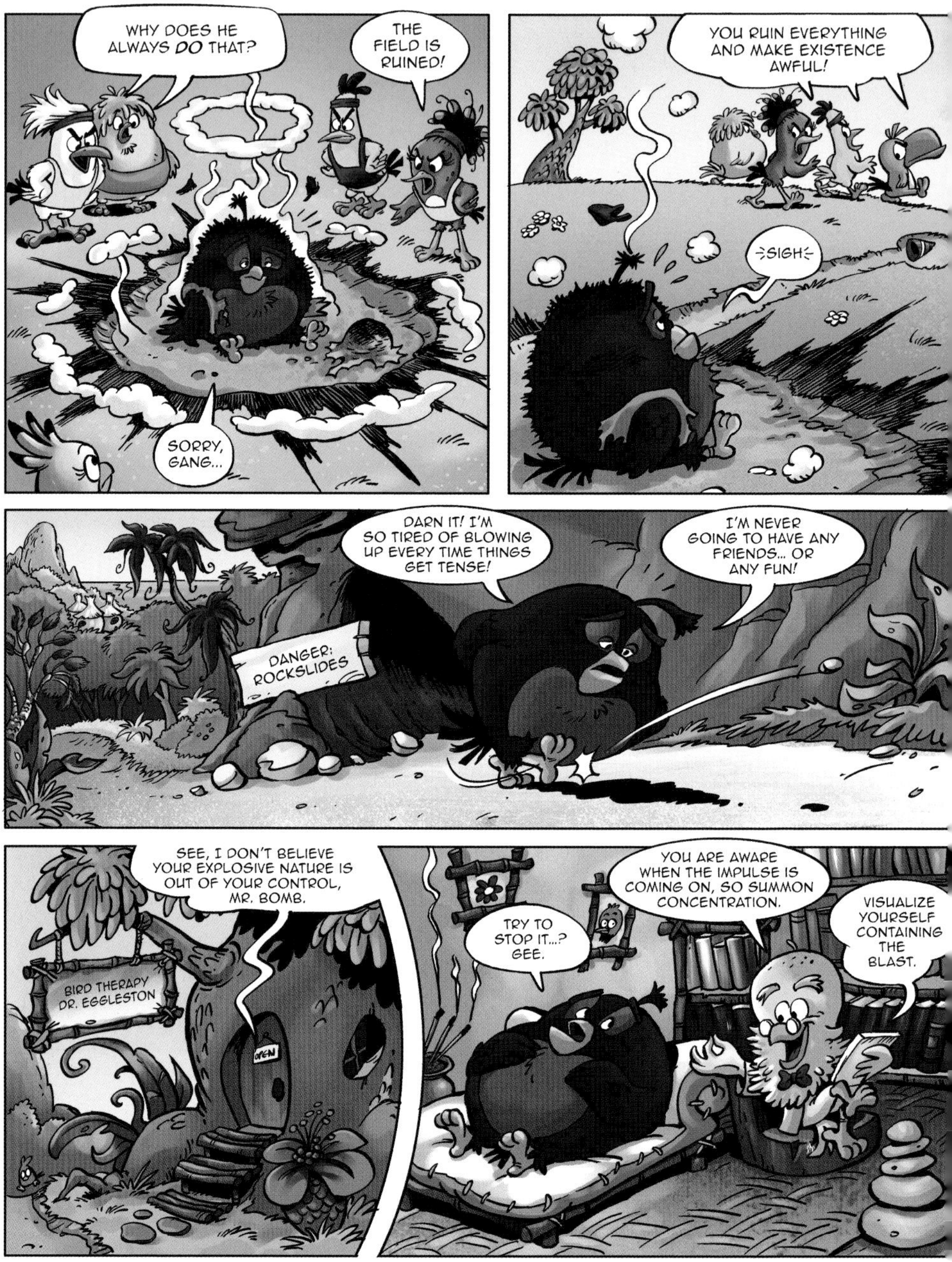
WHY DOES HE ALWAYS *DO* THAT?
THE FIELD IS RUINED!
SORRY, GANG...
YOU RUIN EVERYTHING AND MAKE EXISTENCE AWFUL!
SIGH
DARN IT! I'M SO TIRED OF BLOWING UP EVERY TIME THINGS GET TENSE!
I'M NEVER GOING TO HAVE ANY FRIENDS... OR ANY FUN!
DANGER: ROCKSLIDES
BIRD THERAPY DR. EGGLESTON
SEE, I DON'T BELIEVE YOUR EXPLOSIVE NATURE IS OUT OF YOUR CONTROL, MR. BOMB.
OPEN
TRY TO STOP IT...? GEE.
YOU ARE AWARE WHEN THE IMPULSE IS COMING ON, SO SUMMON CONCENTRATION.
VISUALIZE YOURSELF CONTAINING THE BLAST.

THROUGH THE FOREST THERE WILL BE THE PERFECT PLACE TO PRACTICE... FAR AWAY FROM MY OFFICE!

OKAY DOC, I'LL GIVE IT WHIRL. THANKS!

BUT WHAT'S SO PERFECT ABOUT THIS PART OF THE JUNGLE TO KEEP FROM--

OW!

TOK

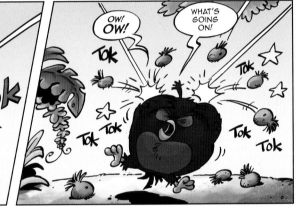

OW! OW!

WHAT'S GOING ON!

TOK

TOK

TOK TOK

TOK

TOK

GRR, YOU LITTLE PUNKS! YOU BETTER STOP!

I'M GETTING PRETTY MAD...

NO-- THIS IS WHAT DOC MEANT!

VISUALIZE, VISUALIZE! ME, NOT BLOWING UP!

HOLD IT IN, DON'T EXPLODE...

HOLD... IT... IN....

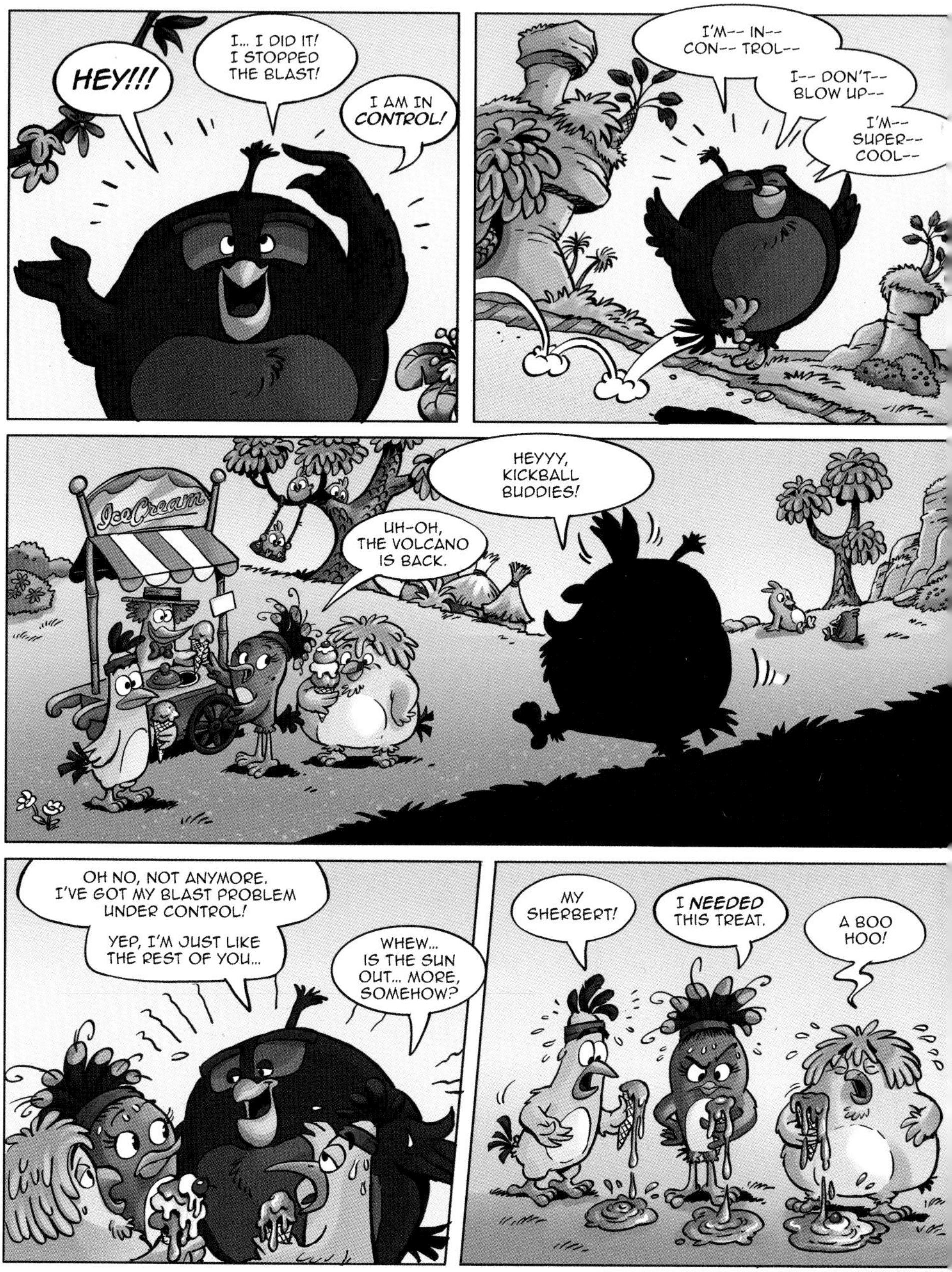
HEY!!!
I... I DID IT! I STOPPED THE BLAST!
I AM IN CONTROL!
I'M-- IN-- CON-- TROL--
I-- DON'T-- BLOW UP--
I'M-- SUPER-- COOL--
HEYYY, KICKBALL BUDDIES!
UH-OH, THE VOLCANO IS BACK.
OH NO, NOT ANYMORE. I'VE GOT MY BLAST PROBLEM UNDER CONTROL!
YEP, I'M JUST LIKE THE REST OF YOU...
WHEW... IS THE SUN OUT... MORE, SOMEHOW?
MY SHERBERT!
I NEEDED THIS TREAT.
A BOO HOO!

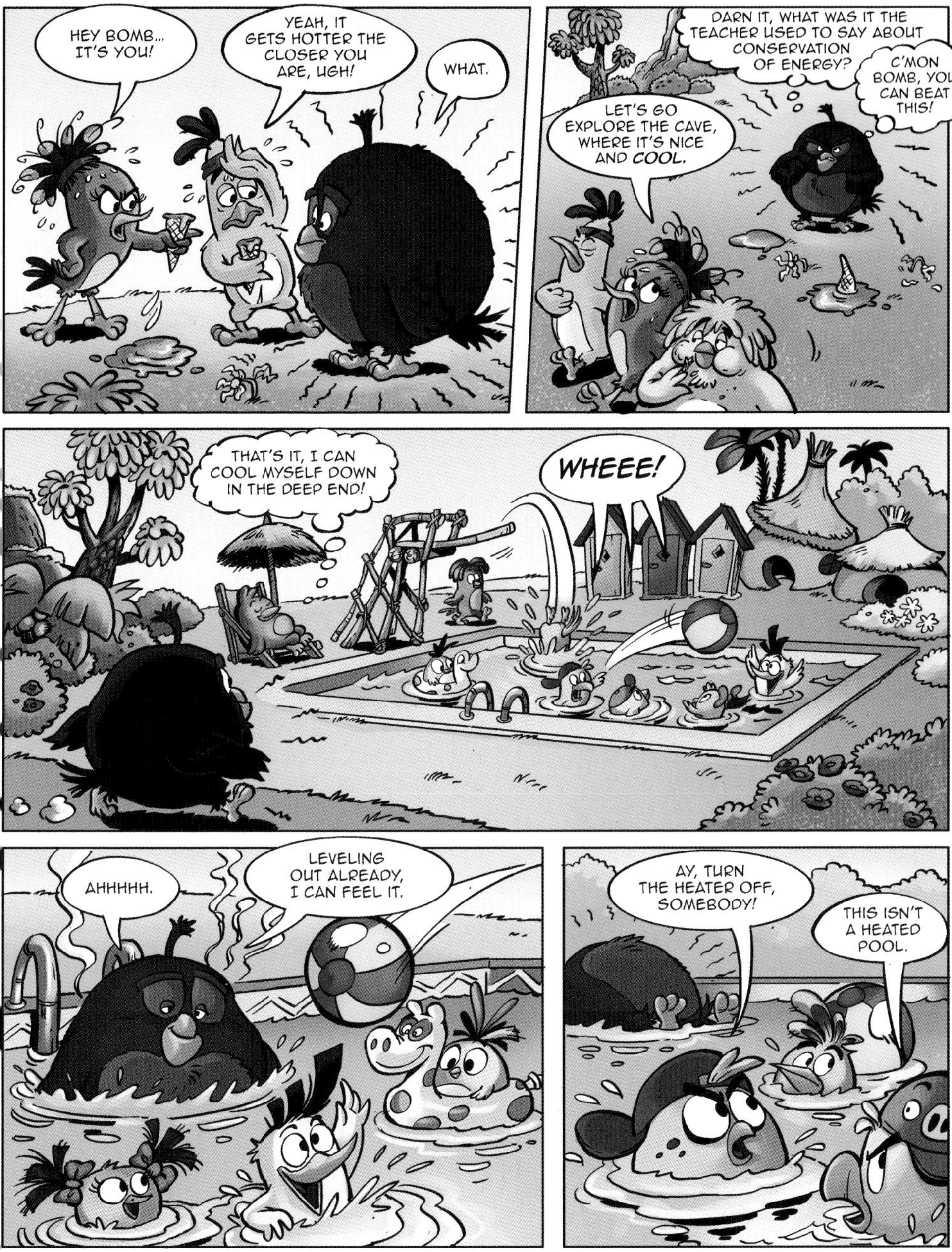
HEY BOMB... IT'S YOU!
YEAH, IT GETS HOTTER THE CLOSER YOU ARE, UGH!
WHAT.
DARN IT, WHAT WAS IT THE TEACHER USED TO SAY ABOUT CONSERVATION OF ENERGY?
C'MON BOMB, YOU CAN BEAT THIS!
LET'S GO EXPLORE THE CAVE, WHERE IT'S NICE AND COOL.
THAT'S IT, I CAN COOL MYSELF DOWN IN THE DEEP END!
WHEEE!
AHHHHH.
LEVELING OUT ALREADY, I CAN FEEL IT.
AY, TURN THE HEATER OFF, SOMEBODY!
THIS ISN'T A HEATED POOL.

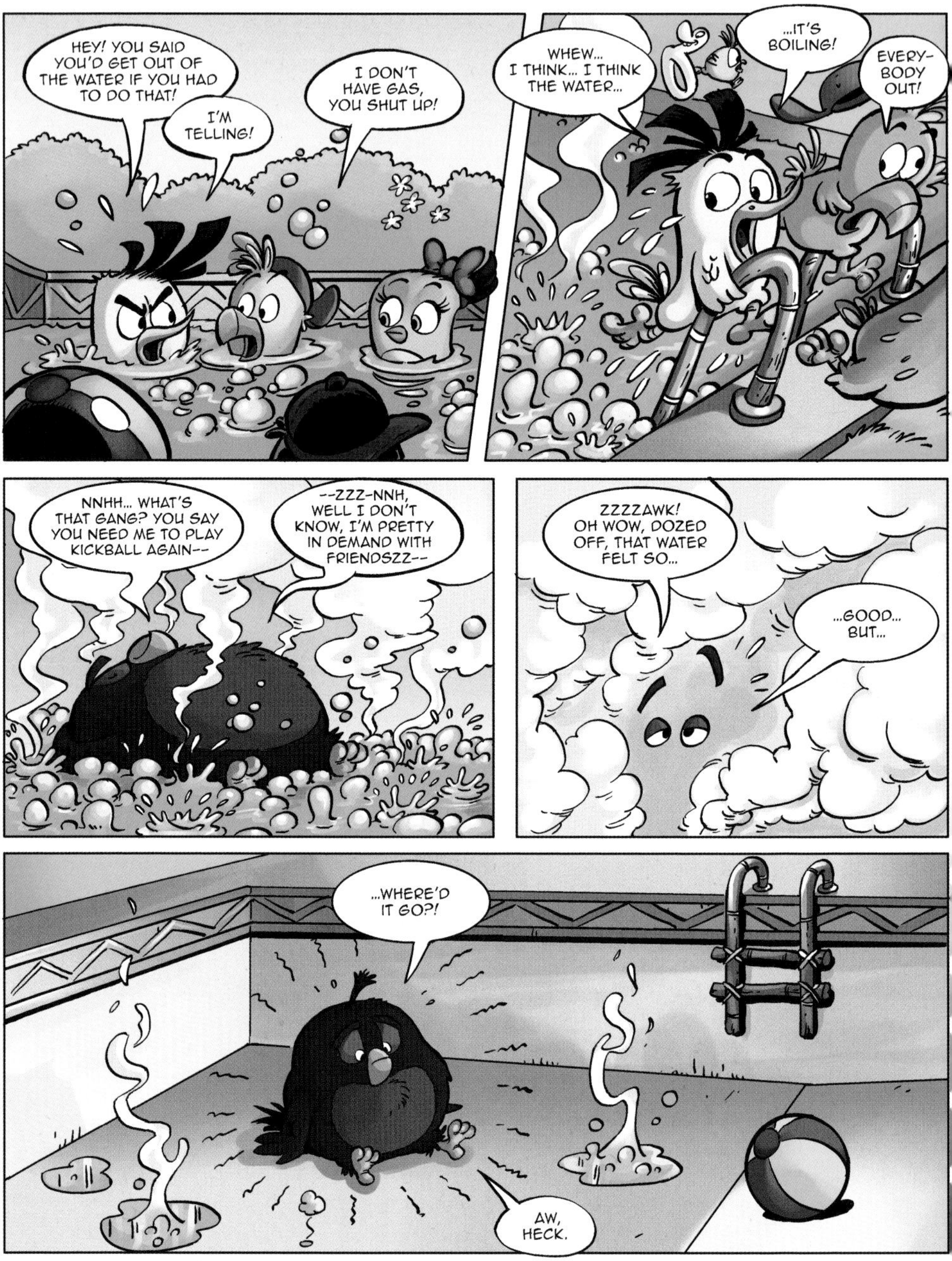

HEY! YOU SAID YOU'D GET OUT OF THE WATER IF YOU HAD TO DO THAT!
I'M TELLING!
I DON'T HAVE GAS, YOU SHUT UP!
WHEW... I THINK... I THINK THE WATER...
...IT'S BOILING!
EVERY-BODY OUT!
NNHH... WHAT'S THAT GANG? YOU SAY YOU NEED ME TO PLAY KICKBALL AGAIN--
--ZZZ-NNH, WELL I DON'T KNOW, I'M PRETTY IN DEMAND WITH FRIENDSZZ--
ZZZZAWK! OH WOW, DOZED OFF, THAT WATER FELT SO...
...GOOD... BUT...
...WHERE'D IT GO?!
AW, HECK.

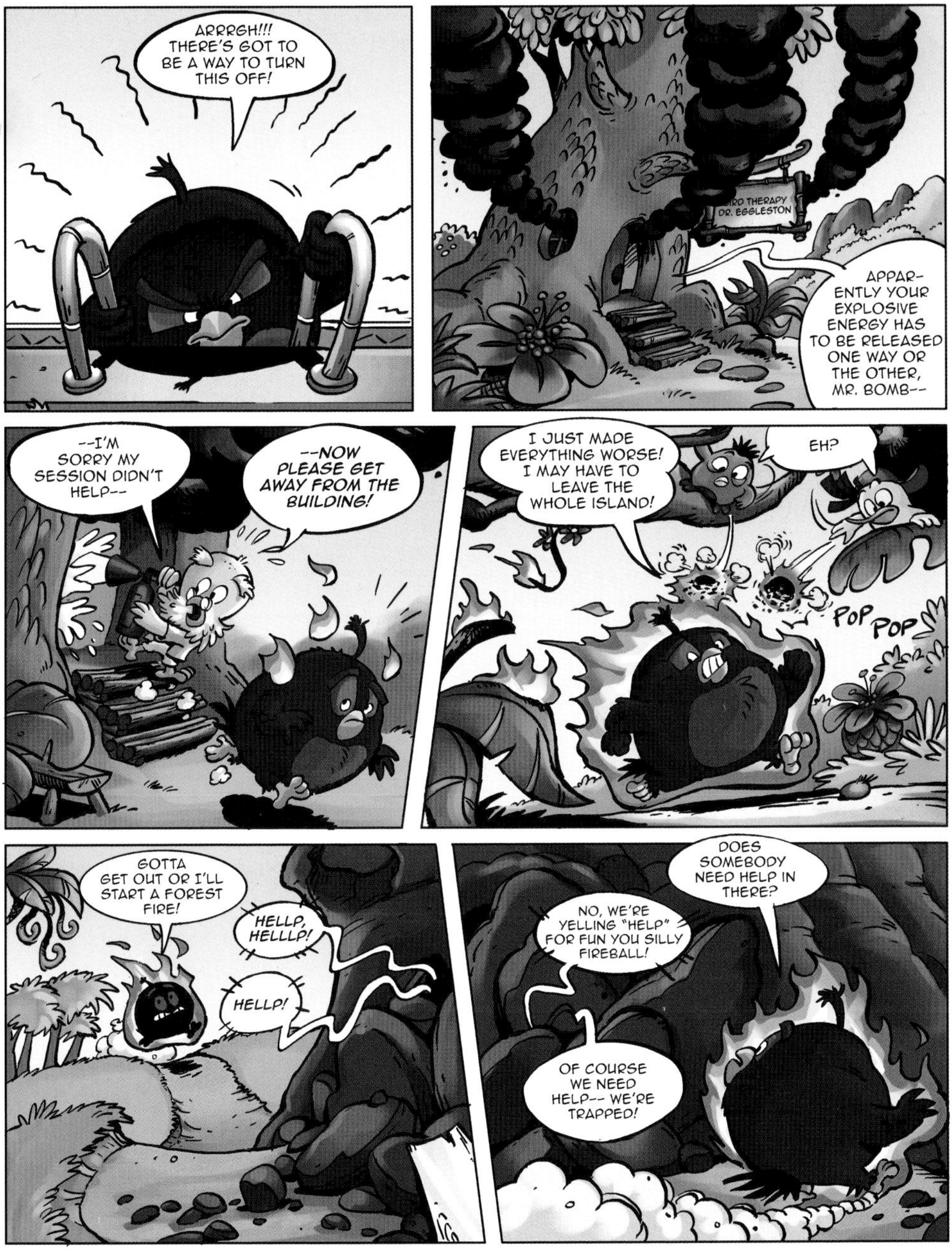
ARRRGH!!! THERE'S GOT TO BE A WAY TO TURN THIS OFF!
BIRD THERAPY DR. EGGLESTON
APPAR-ENTLY YOUR EXPLOSIVE ENERGY HAS TO BE RELEASED ONE WAY OR THE OTHER, MR. BOMB--
--I'M SORRY MY SESSION DIDN'T HELP--
--NOW PLEASE GET AWAY FROM THE BUILDING!
I JUST MADE EVERYTHING WORSE! I MAY HAVE TO LEAVE THE WHOLE ISLAND!
EH?
POP POP
GOTTA GET OUT OR I'LL START A FOREST FIRE!
HELLP, HELLLP!
HELLP!
DOES SOMEBODY NEED HELP IN THERE?
NO, WE'RE YELLING "HELP" FOR FUN YOU SILLY FIREBALL!
OF COURSE WE NEED HELP-- WE'RE TRAPPED!

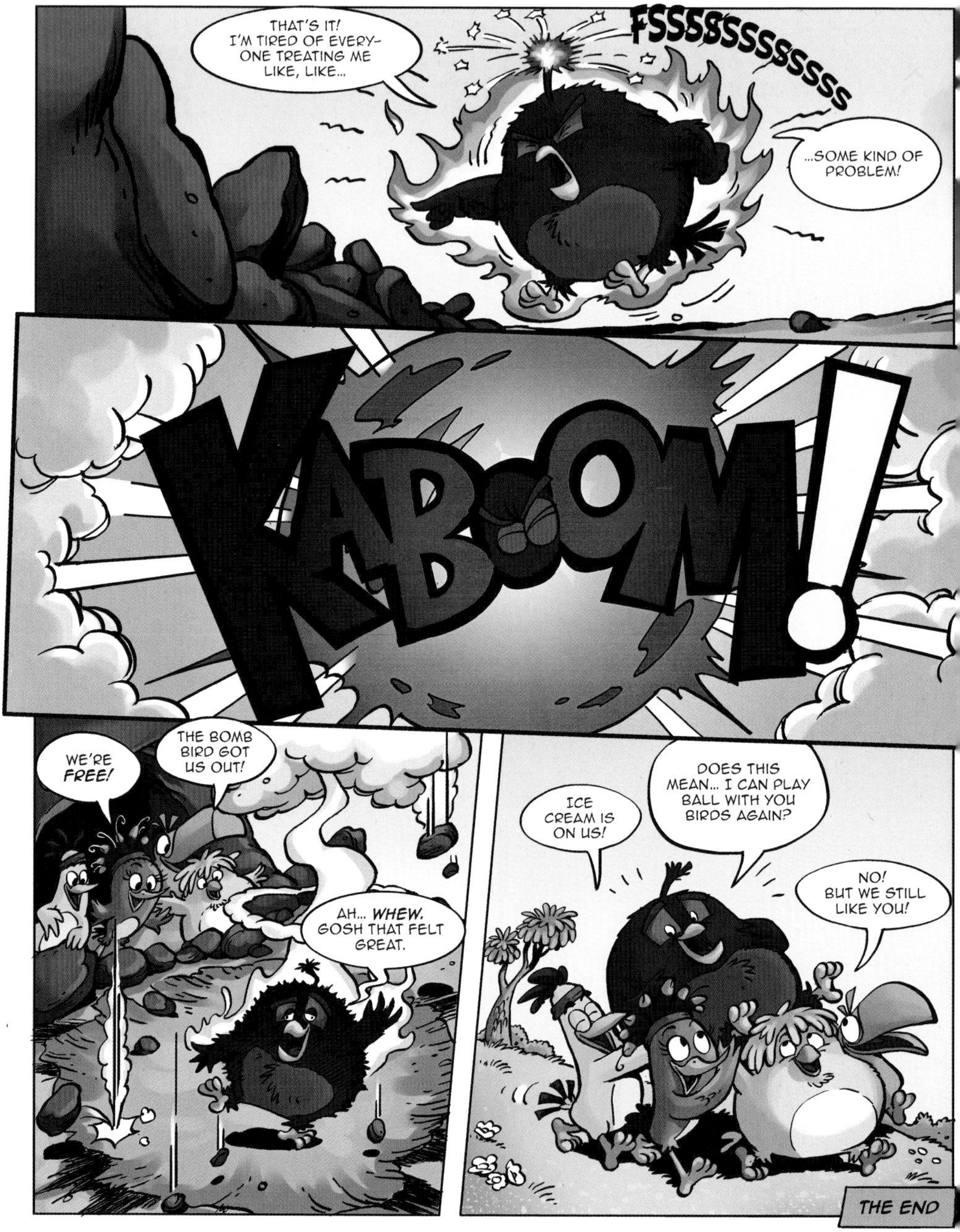
THAT'S IT! I'M TIRED OF EVERYONE TREATING ME LIKE, LIKE...
FSSSSSSSSSSSSS
...SOME KIND OF PROBLEM!
KABOOM!
WE'RE FREE!
THE BOMB BIRD GOT US OUT!
AH... WHEW. GOSH THAT FELT GREAT.
ICE CREAM IS ON US!
DOES THIS MEAN... I CAN PLAY BALL WITH YOU BIRDS AGAIN?
NO! BUT WE STILL LIKE YOU!
THE END

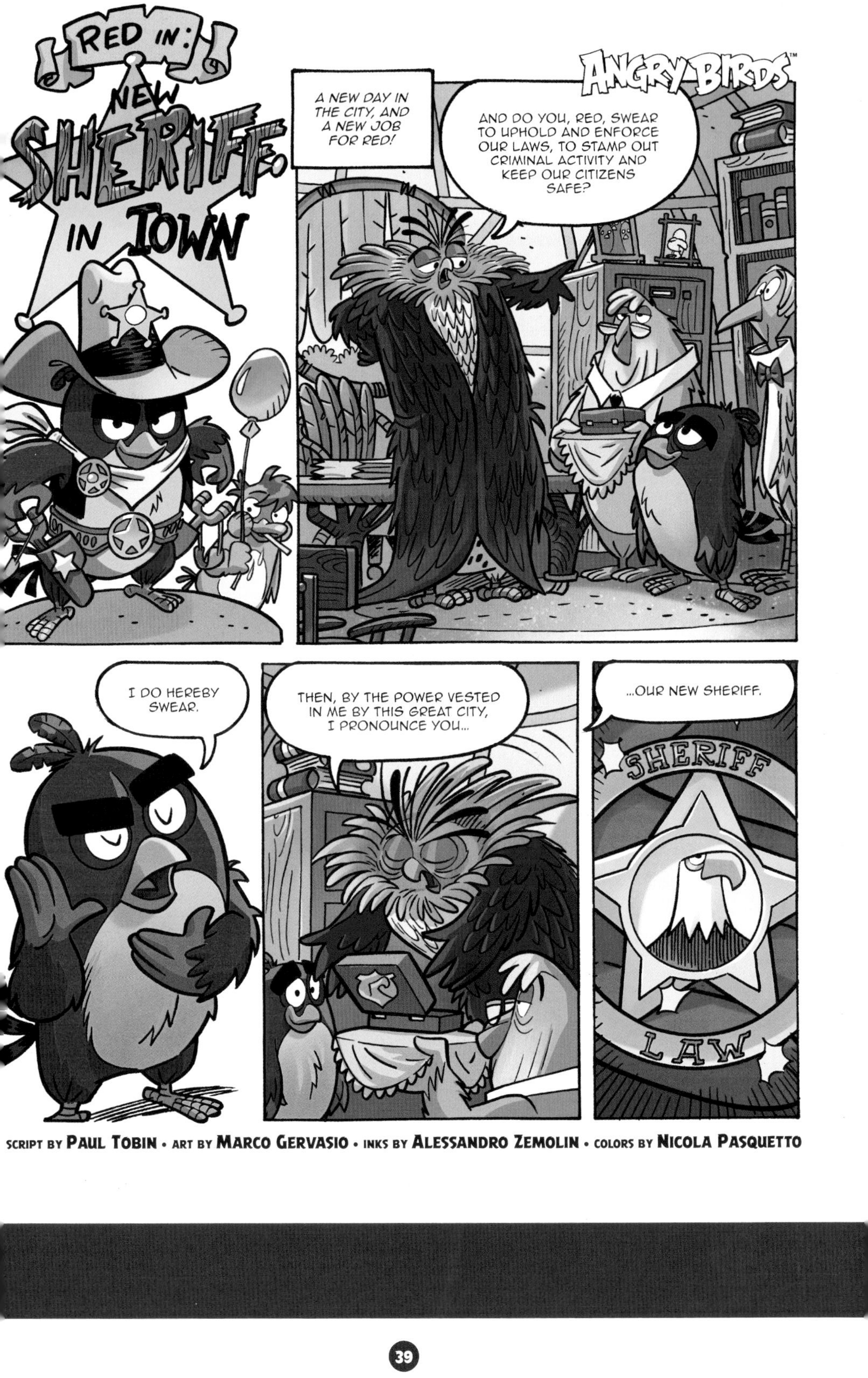
RED IN:
NEW SHERIFF IN TOWN
ANGRY BIRDS
A NEW DAY IN THE CITY, AND A NEW JOB FOR RED!
AND DO YOU, RED, SWEAR TO UPHOLD AND ENFORCE OUR LAWS, TO STAMP OUT CRIMINAL ACTIVITY AND KEEP OUR CITIZENS SAFE?
I DO HEREBY SWEAR.
THEN, BY THE POWER VESTED IN ME BY THIS GREAT CITY, I PRONOUNCE YOU...
...OUR NEW SHERIFF.
SHERIFF
LAW

SCRIPT BY **PAUL TOBIN** • ART BY **MARCO GERVASIO** • INKS BY **ALESSANDRO ZEMOLIN** • COLORS BY **NICOLA PASQUETTO**

[redacted]

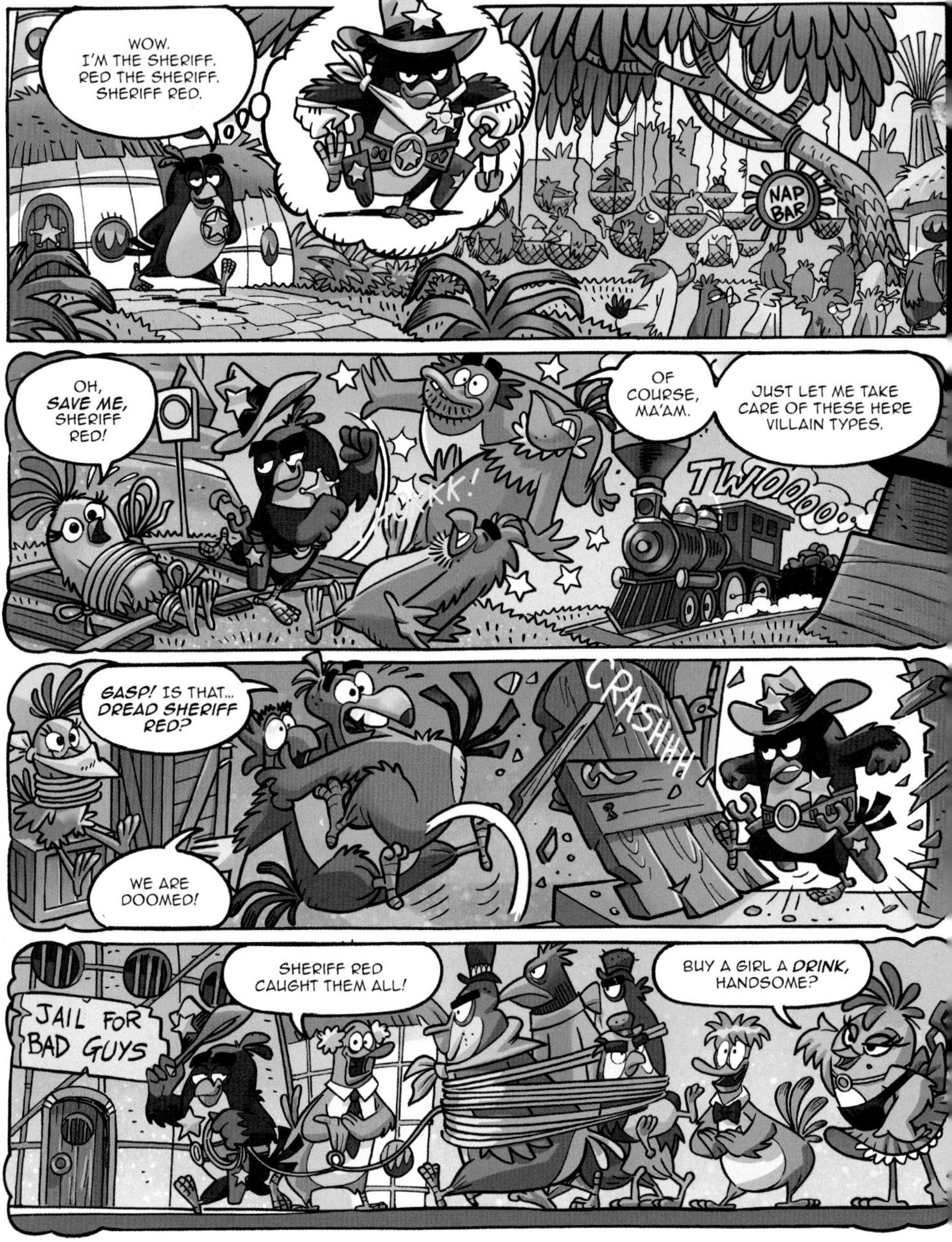
WOW. I'M THE SHERIFF. RED THE SHERIFF. SHERIFF RED.
NAP BAR
OH, *SAVE ME,* SHERIFF RED!
OF COURSE, MA'AM.
JUST LET ME TAKE CARE OF THESE HERE VILLAIN TYPES.
TWOOOOO..
GASP! IS THAT... *DREAD SHERIFF RED?*
WE ARE DOOMED!
CRASHHH
SHERIFF RED CAUGHT THEM ALL!
BUY A GIRL A *DRINK,* HANDSOME?
JAIL FOR BAD GUYS

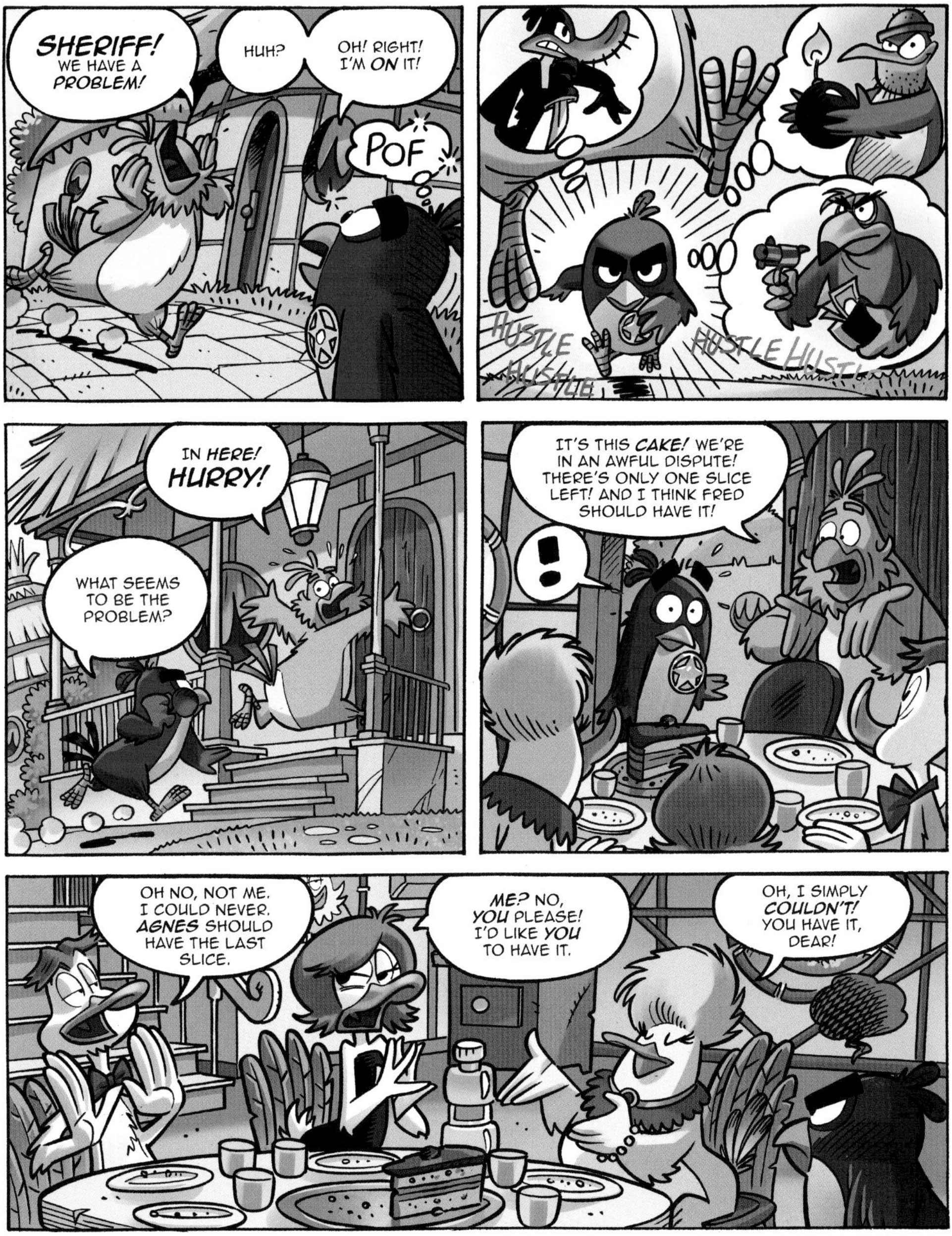

SHERIFF! WE HAVE A PROBLEM!
HUH?
OH! RIGHT! I'M ON IT!
POF
HUSTLE HUSTLE
HUSTLE HUSTLE
IN HERE! HURRY!
WHAT SEEMS TO BE THE PROBLEM?
IT'S THIS CAKE! WE'RE IN AN AWFUL DISPUTE! THERE'S ONLY ONE SLICE LEFT! AND I THINK FRED SHOULD HAVE IT!
!
OH NO, NOT ME. I COULD NEVER. AGNES SHOULD HAVE THE LAST SLICE.
ME? NO, YOU PLEASE! I'D LIKE YOU TO HAVE IT.
OH, I SIMPLY COULDN'T! YOU HAVE IT, DEAR!

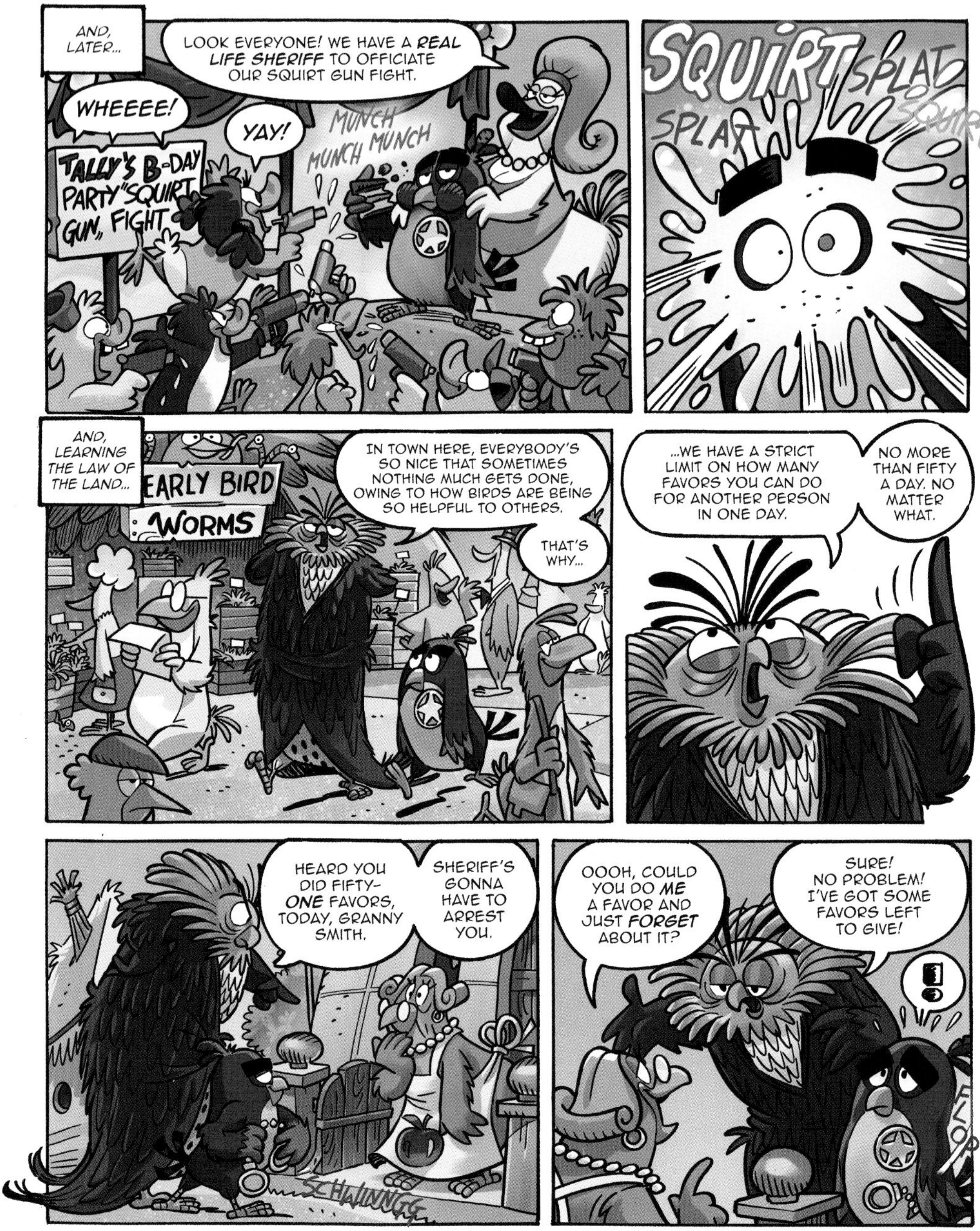
AND, LATER...
LOOK EVERYONE! WE HAVE A REAL LIFE SHERIFF TO OFFICIATE OUR SQUIRT GUN FIGHT.
WHEEEE!
YAY!
MUNCH MUNCH MUNCH
TALLY'S B-DAY PARTY "SQUIRT GUN" FIGHT
SQUIRT SPLAT SPLAT SQUIRT
AND, LEARNING THE LAW OF THE LAND...
EARLY BIRD WORMS
IN TOWN HERE, EVERYBODY'S SO NICE THAT SOMETIMES NOTHING MUCH GETS DONE, OWING TO HOW BIRDS ARE BEING SO HELPFUL TO OTHERS.
THAT'S WHY...
...WE HAVE A STRICT LIMIT ON HOW MANY FAVORS YOU CAN DO FOR ANOTHER PERSON IN ONE DAY.
NO MORE THAN FIFTY A DAY. NO MATTER WHAT.
HEARD YOU DID FIFTY-ONE FAVORS, TODAY, GRANNY SMITH.
SHERIFF'S GONNA HAVE TO ARREST YOU.
SCHWINNGG
OOOH, COULD YOU DO ME A FAVOR AND JUST FORGET ABOUT IT?
SURE! NO PROBLEM! I'VE GOT SOME FAVORS LEFT TO GIVE!
FLOP

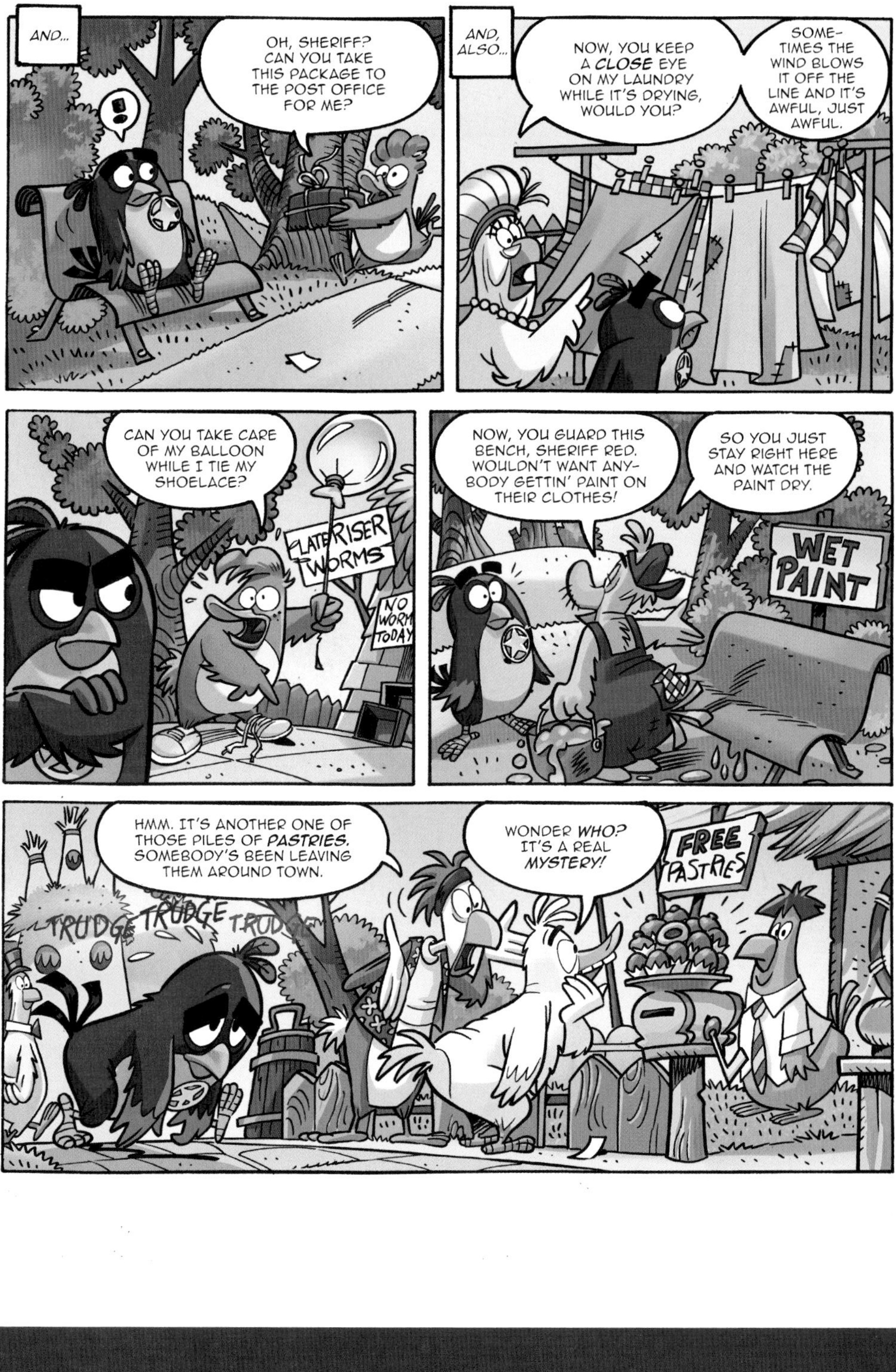
AND...
OH, SHERIFF? CAN YOU TAKE THIS PACKAGE TO THE POST OFFICE FOR ME?
AND, ALSO...
NOW, YOU KEEP A *CLOSE* EYE ON MY LAUNDRY WHILE IT'S DRYING, WOULD YOU?
SOMETIMES THE WIND BLOWS IT OFF THE LINE AND IT'S AWFUL, JUST AWFUL.
CAN YOU TAKE CARE OF MY BALLOON WHILE I TIE MY SHOELACE?
LATE RISER WORMS
NO WORMS TODAY
NOW, YOU GUARD THIS BENCH, SHERIFF RED. WOULDN'T WANT ANYBODY GETTIN' PAINT ON THEIR CLOTHES!
SO YOU JUST STAY RIGHT HERE AND WATCH THE PAINT DRY.
WET PAINT
HMM. IT'S ANOTHER ONE OF THOSE PILES OF *PASTRIES.* SOMEBODY'S BEEN LEAVING THEM AROUND TOWN.
WONDER *WHO?* IT'S A REAL *MYSTERY!*
FREE PASTRIES
TRUDGE TRUDGE TRUDGE

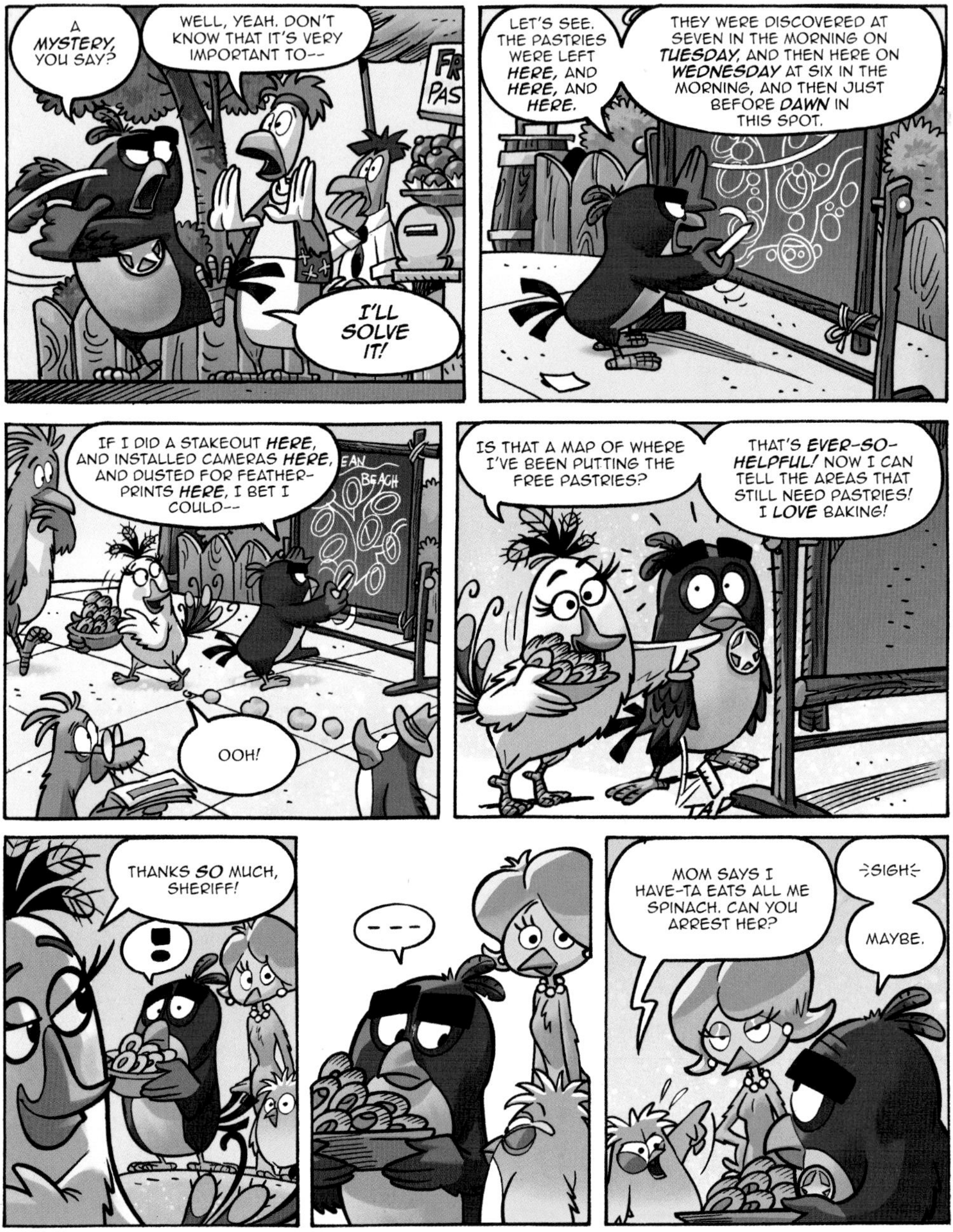

A MYSTERY, YOU SAY?
WELL, YEAH. DON'T KNOW THAT IT'S VERY IMPORTANT TO--
I'LL SOLVE IT!
LET'S SEE. THE PASTRIES WERE LEFT HERE, AND HERE, AND HERE.
THEY WERE DISCOVERED AT SEVEN IN THE MORNING ON TUESDAY, AND THEN HERE ON WEDNESDAY AT SIX IN THE MORNING, AND THEN JUST BEFORE DAWN IN THIS SPOT.
IF I DID A STAKEOUT HERE, AND INSTALLED CAMERAS HERE, AND DUSTED FOR FEATHER-PRINTS HERE, I BET I COULD--
OOH!
IS THAT A MAP OF WHERE I'VE BEEN PUTTING THE FREE PASTRIES?
THAT'S EVER-SO-HELPFUL! NOW I CAN TELL THE AREAS THAT STILL NEED PASTRIES! I LOVE BAKING!
TAP
THANKS SO MUCH, SHERIFF!
!
- - -
MOM SAYS I HAVE-TA EATS ALL ME SPINACH. CAN YOU ARREST HER?
SIGH
MAYBE.

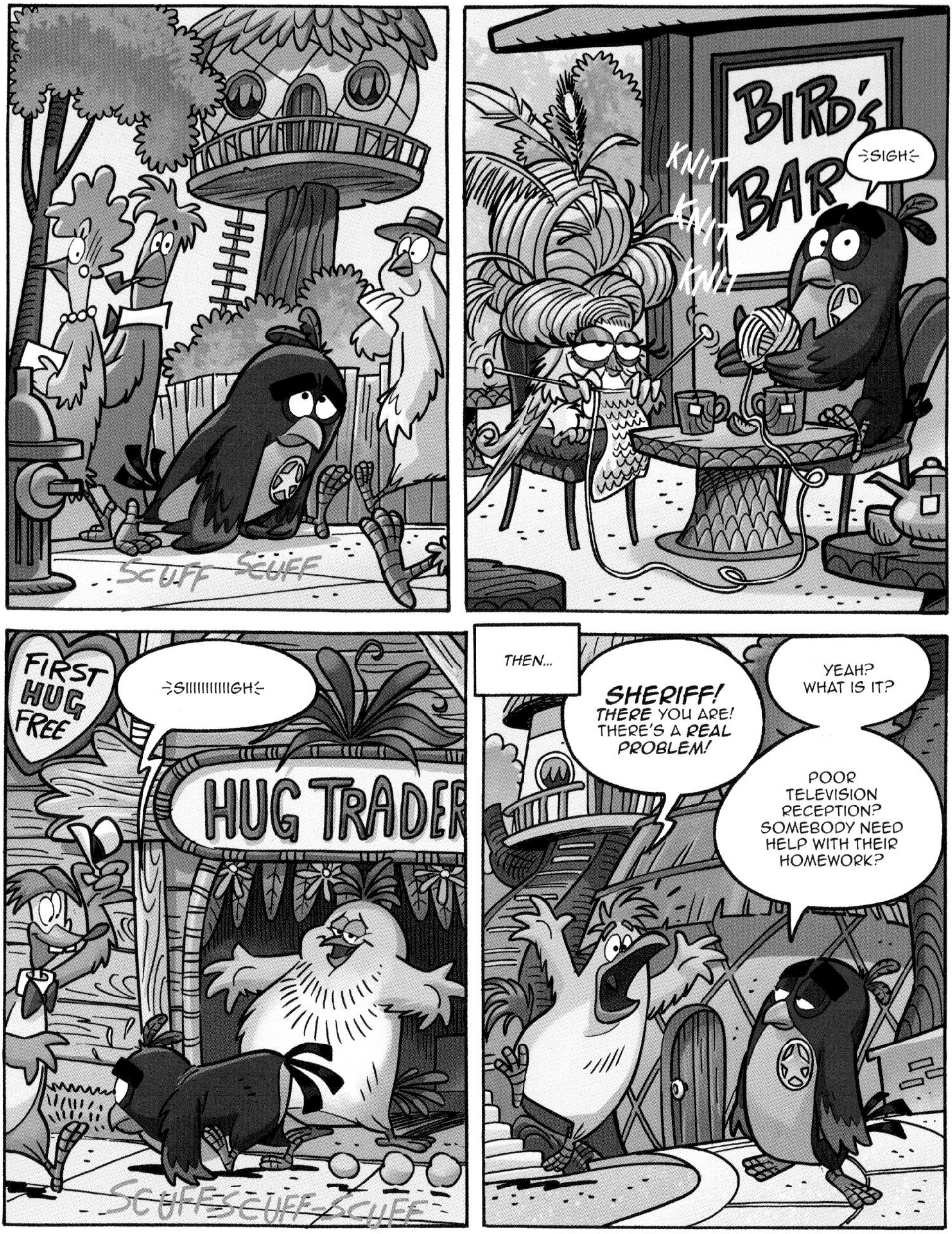
SCUFF SCUFF
BIRD'S BAR
KNIT KNIT KNIT
-SIGH-
FIRST HUG FREE
-SIIIIIIIIIIGH-
HUG TRADER
SCUFF-SCUFF-SCUFF
THEN...
SHERIFF! THERE YOU ARE! THERE'S A REAL PROBLEM!
YEAH? WHAT IS IT?
POOR TELEVISION RECEPTION? SOMEBODY NEED HELP WITH THEIR HOMEWORK?

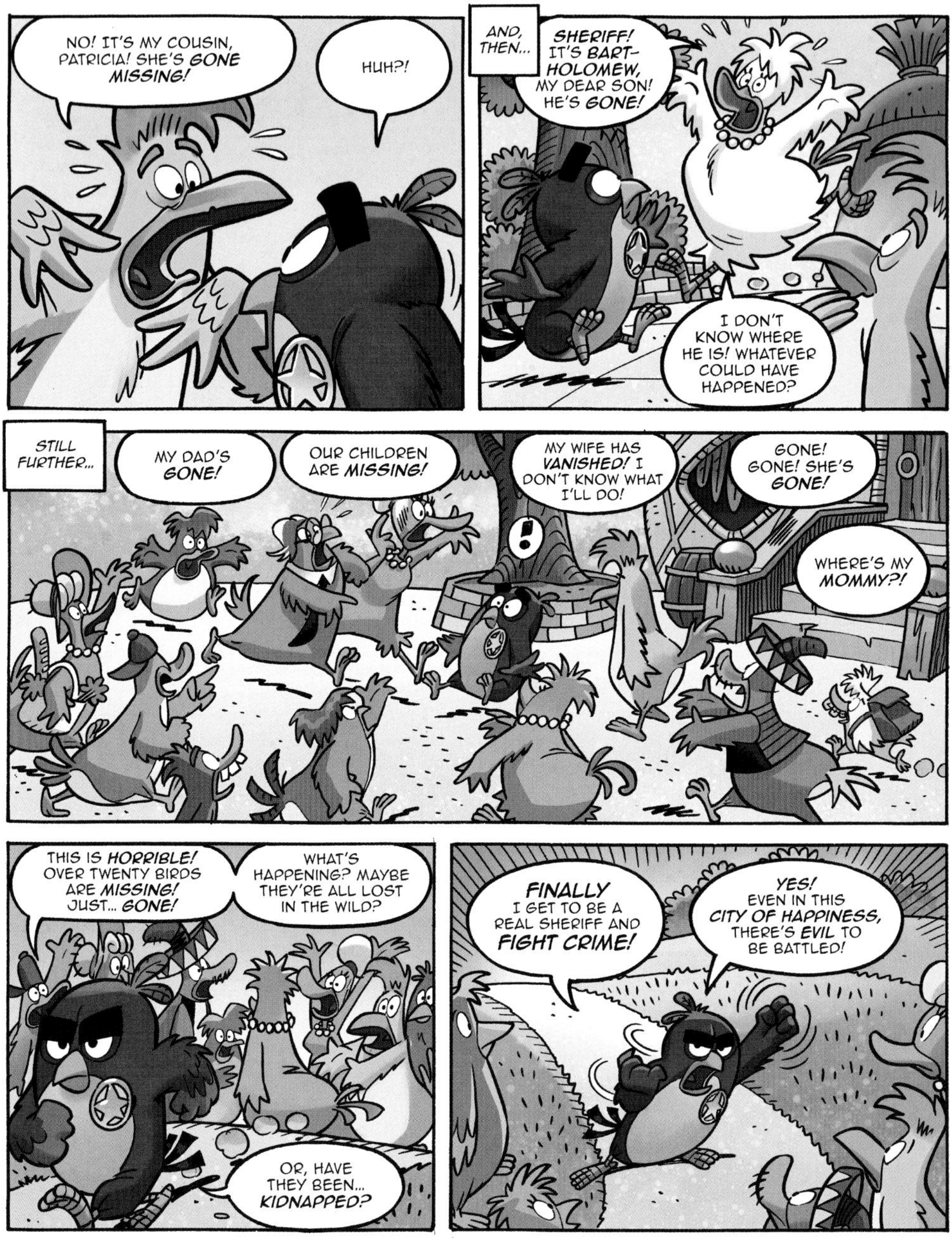

NO! IT'S MY COUSIN, PATRICIA! SHE'S GONE MISSING!
HUH?!
AND, THEN...
SHERIFF! IT'S BART-HOLOMEW, MY DEAR SON! HE'S GONE!
I DON'T KNOW WHERE HE IS! WHATEVER COULD HAVE HAPPENED?
STILL FURTHER...
MY DAD'S GONE!
OUR CHILDREN ARE MISSING!
MY WIFE HAS VANISHED! I DON'T KNOW WHAT I'LL DO!
GONE! GONE! SHE'S GONE!
WHERE'S MY MOMMY?!
THIS IS HORRIBLE! OVER TWENTY BIRDS ARE MISSING! JUST... GONE!
WHAT'S HAPPENING? MAYBE THEY'RE ALL LOST IN THE WILD?
OR, HAVE THEY BEEN... KIDNAPPED?
FINALLY I GET TO BE A REAL SHERIFF AND FIGHT CRIME!
YES! EVEN IN THIS CITY OF HAPPINESS, THERE'S EVIL TO BE BATTLED!

HMM.

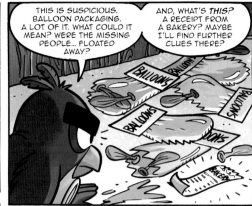

THIS IS SUSPICIOUS. BALLOON PACKAGING. A LOT OF IT. WHAT COULD IT MEAN? WERE THE MISSING PEOPLE... FLOATED AWAY?

AND, WHAT'S *THIS*? A RECEIPT FROM A BAKERY? MAYBE I'LL FIND FURTHER CLUES THERE?

FEATERCRUST BAKERY

CLOSED. SO SORRY

CAKES SO LIGHT THEY'LL **FLOAT** AWAY!

CLOSED? ON A WEEKDAY?

BIRD MAIL

THAT'S INTERESTING.

WHA... *EVERYONE'S* GONE, NOW?

THIS IS GETTING OUT OF CONTROL! WHO'S ABDUCTING THEM?

BIRD COURT

MUSIC FROM IN HERE? VOICES? THE KIDNAPPERS?

OKAY! TIME TO GO IN *HARD*, RED!

NO TELLING WHAT *DANGERS* I'M ABOUT TO FACE!

THIS IS A *RELENTLESS* BATTLE AGAINST THE *FORCES* OF...

SBAM

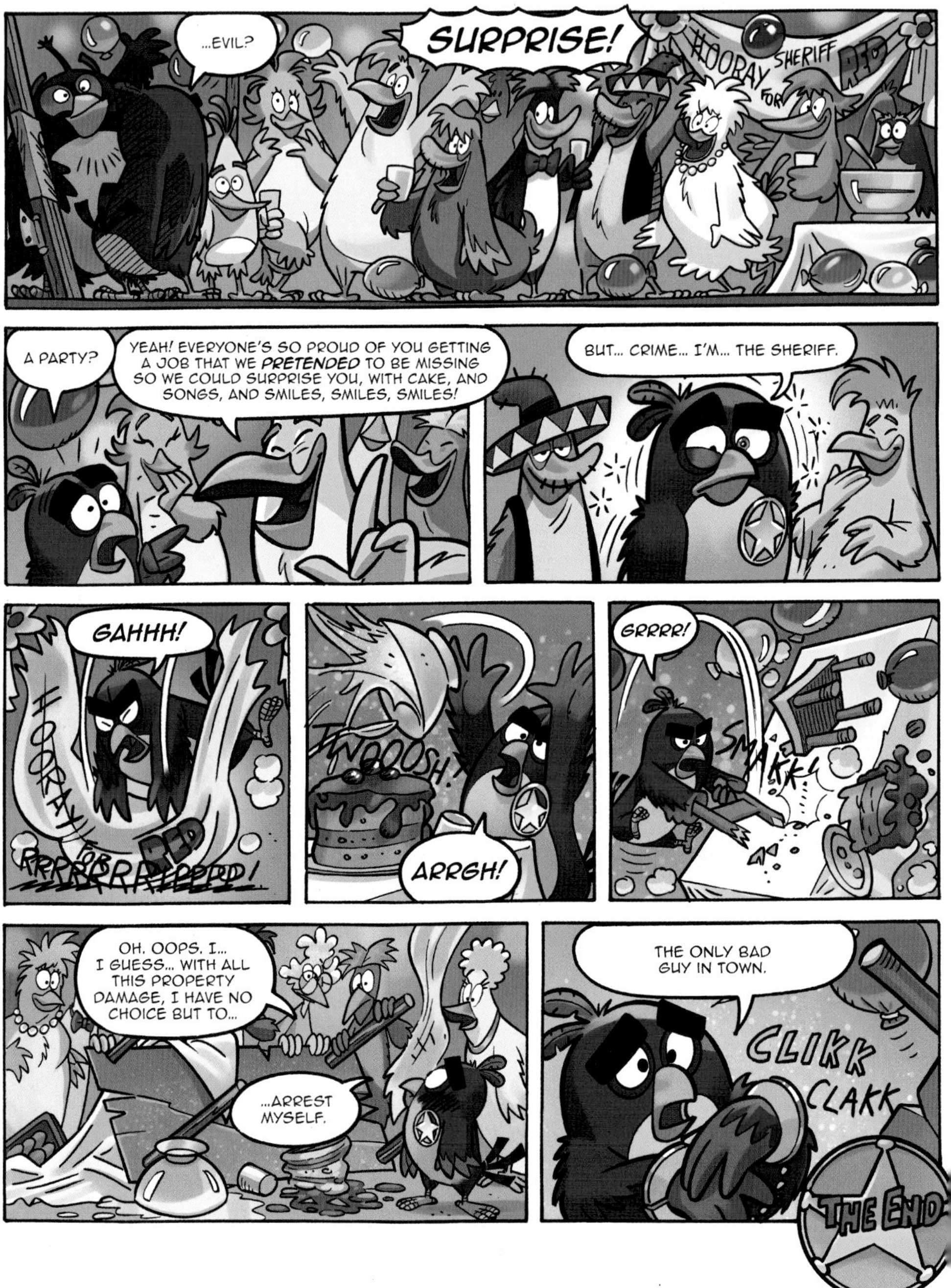
...EVIL?
SURPRISE!
HOORAY FOR SHERIFF RED
A PARTY?
YEAH! EVERYONE'S SO PROUD OF YOU GETTING A JOB THAT WE *PRETENDED* TO BE MISSING SO WE COULD SURPRISE YOU, WITH CAKE, AND SONGS, AND SMILES, SMILES, SMILES!
BUT... CRIME... I'M... THE SHERIFF.
GAHHH!
RRRRRRRRIPPPP!
WOOOOSH!
ARRGH!
GRRRR!
SMAKK!
OH. OOPS. I... I GUESS... WITH ALL THIS PROPERTY DAMAGE, I HAVE NO CHOICE BUT TO...
...ARREST MYSELF.
THE ONLY BAD GUY IN TOWN.
CLIKK
CLAKK
THE END

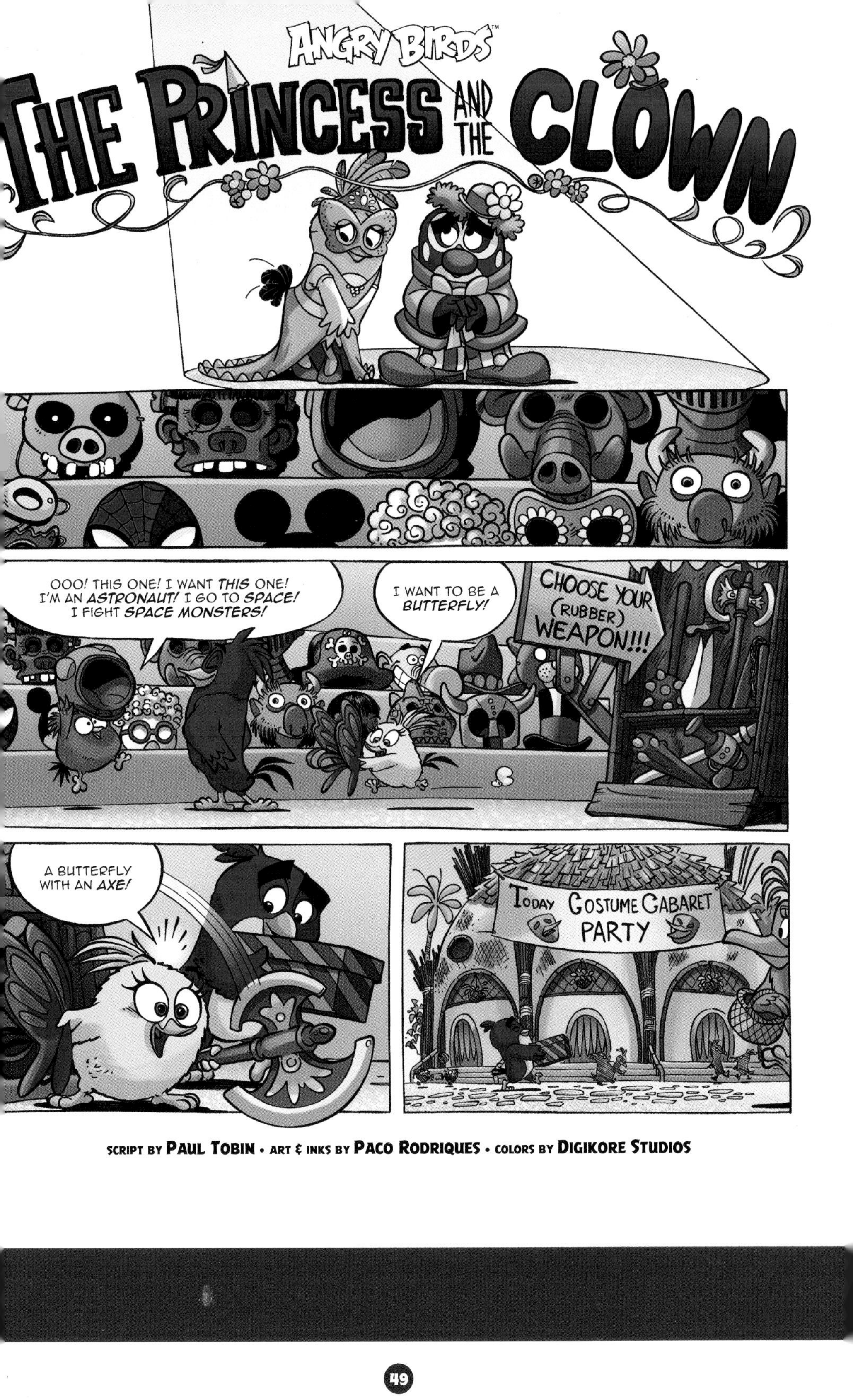
ANGRY BIRDS™
THE PRINCESS AND THE CLOWN
OOO! THIS ONE! I WANT THIS ONE! I'M AN ASTRONAUT! I GO TO SPACE! I FIGHT SPACE MONSTERS!
I WANT TO BE A BUTTERFLY!
CHOOSE YOUR (RUBBER) WEAPON!!!
A BUTTERFLY WITH AN AXE!
TODAY COSTUME CABARET PARTY

SCRIPT BY **PAUL TOBIN** • ART & INKS BY **PACO RODRIQUES** • COLORS BY **DIGIKORE STUDIOS**

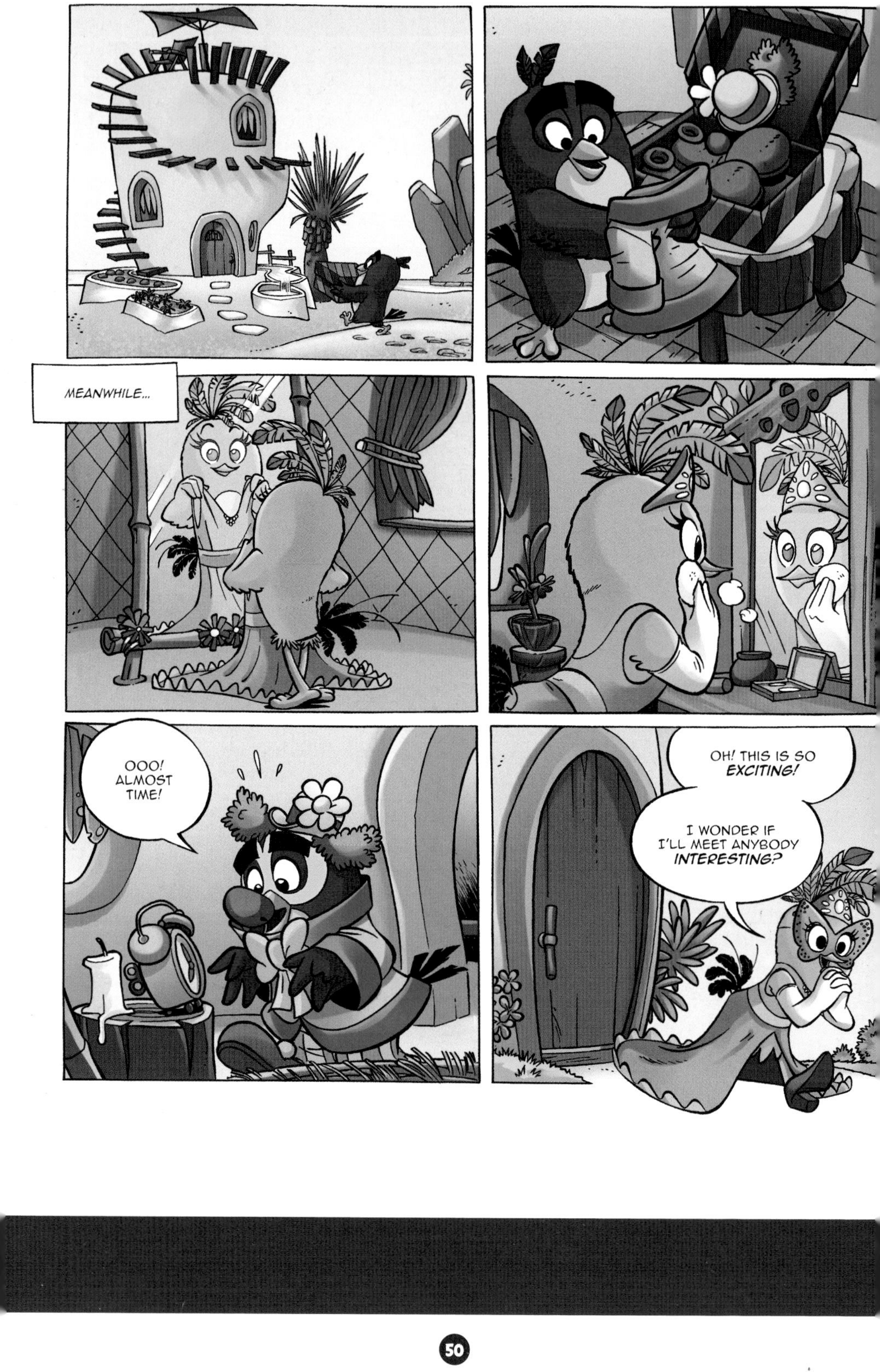
MEANWHILE...
OOO! ALMOST TIME!
OH! THIS IS SO EXCITING!
I WONDER IF I'LL MEET ANYBODY INTERESTING?

HELLO, HELLO! OH, NICELY DONE!

A SCARECROW? MARVELOUS!

OH, IT'S MR. PUMPKIN!

ARE YOU A MAD SCIENTIST? TELL ME OF YOUR CREATIONS!

THE KING! THE KING! MAKE WAY FOR THE KING!

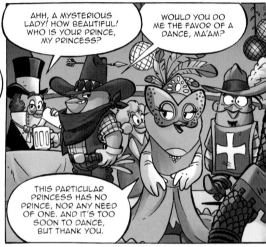

AHH, A MYSTERIOUS LADY! HOW BEAUTIFUL! WHO IS YOUR PRINCE, MY PRINCESS?

WOULD YOU DO ME THE FAVOR OF A DANCE, MA'AM?

THIS PARTICULAR PRINCESS HAS NO PRINCE, NOR ANY NEED OF ONE. AND IT'S TOO SOON TO DANCE, BUT THANK YOU.

STUPID NOSE.

OH, THIS TIARA WON'T SIT STILL.

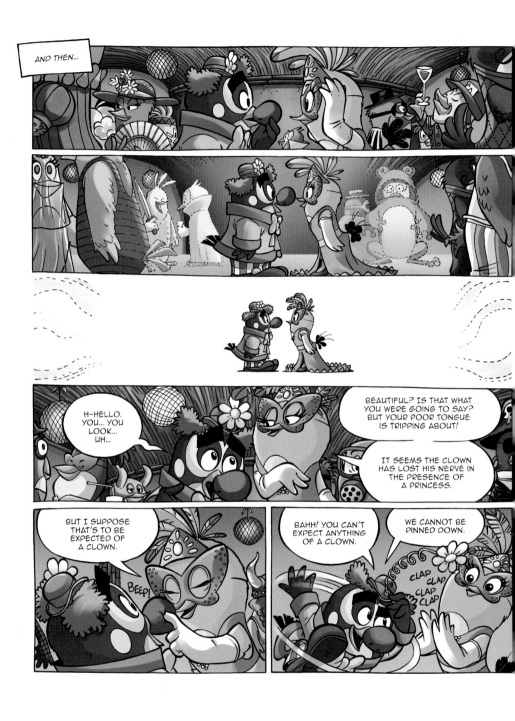

H-HELLO. YOU... YOU LOOK... UH...

BEAUTIFUL? IS THAT WHAT YOU WERE GOING TO SAY? BUT YOUR POOR TONGUE IS TRIPPING ABOUT!

IT SEEMS THE CLOWN HAS LOST HIS NERVE IN THE PRESENCE OF A PRINCESS.

BUT I SUPPOSE THAT'S TO BE EXPECTED OF A CLOWN.

BEEP!

BAHH! YOU CAN'T EXPECT ANYTHING OF A CLOWN.

WE CANNOT BE PINNED DOWN.

CLAP CLAP CLAP CLAP

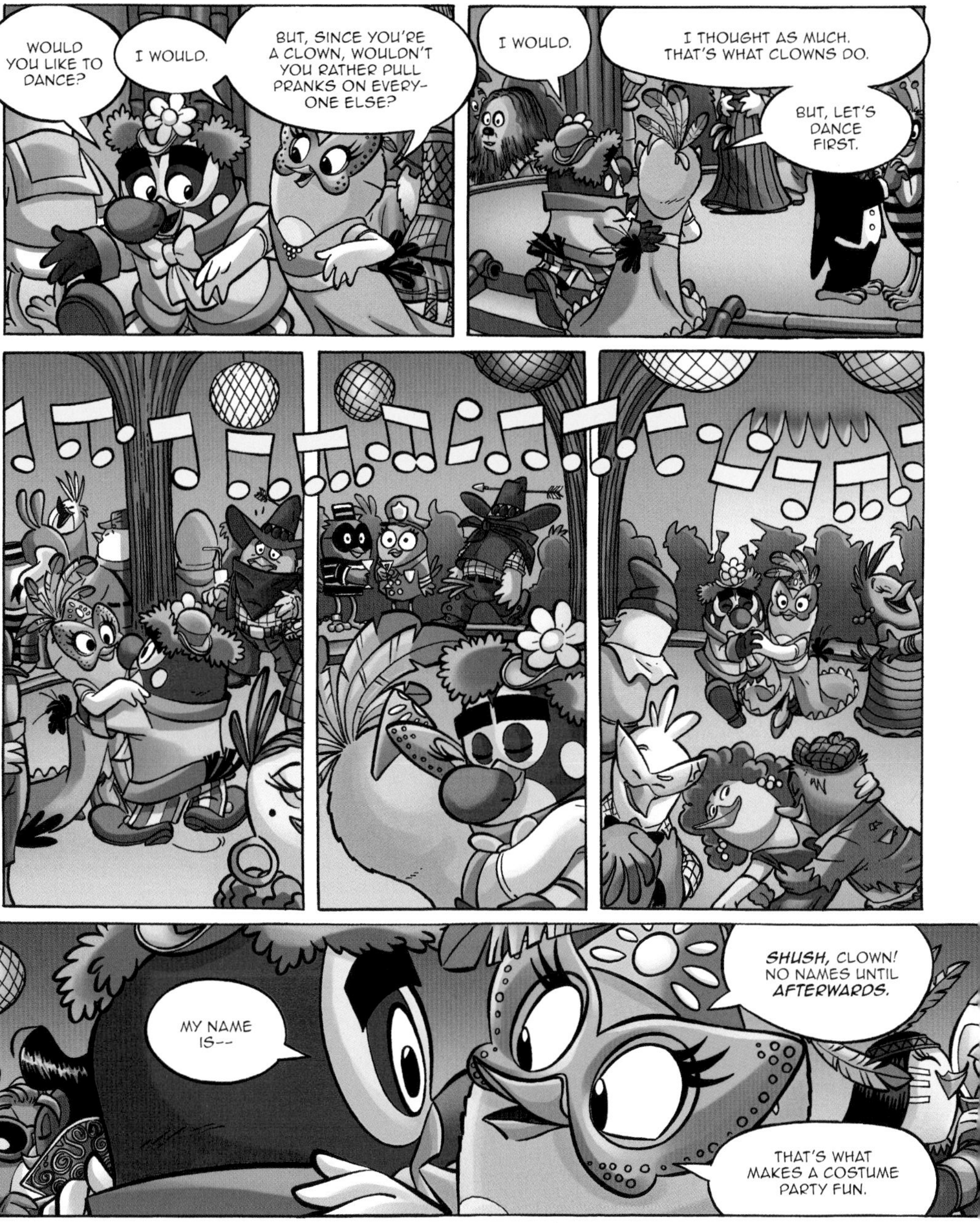
WOULD YOU LIKE TO DANCE?
I WOULD.
BUT, SINCE YOU'RE A CLOWN, WOULDN'T YOU RATHER PULL PRANKS ON EVERY-ONE ELSE?
I WOULD.
I THOUGHT AS MUCH. THAT'S WHAT CLOWNS DO.
BUT, LET'S DANCE FIRST.
MY NAME IS--
SHUSH, CLOWN! NO NAMES UNTIL AFTERWARDS.
THAT'S WHAT MAKES A COSTUME PARTY FUN.

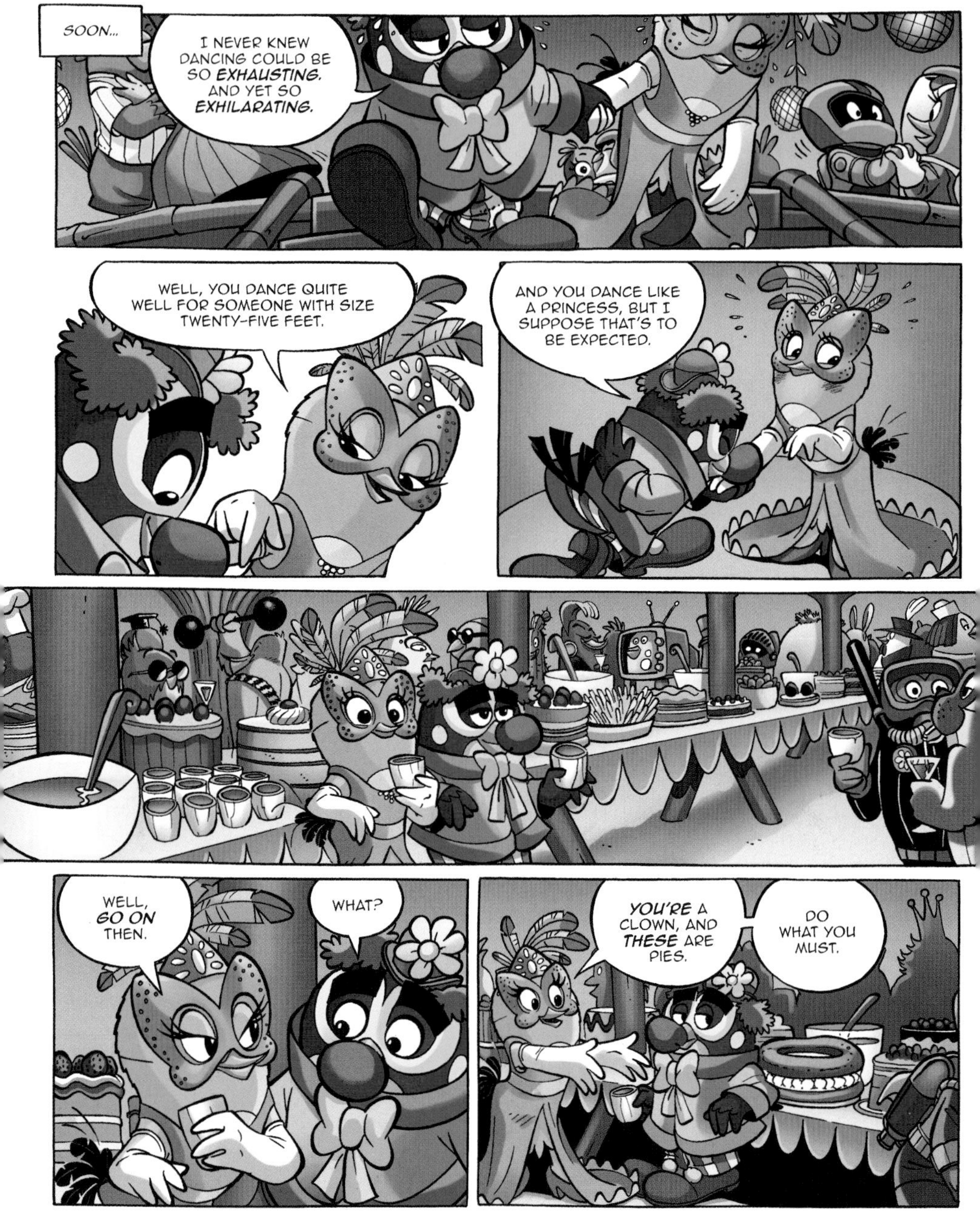
SOON...
I NEVER KNEW DANCING COULD BE SO EXHAUSTING. AND YET SO EXHILARATING.
WELL, YOU DANCE QUITE WELL FOR SOMEONE WITH SIZE TWENTY-FIVE FEET.
AND YOU DANCE LIKE A PRINCESS, BUT I SUPPOSE THAT'S TO BE EXPECTED.
WELL, GO ON THEN.
WHAT?
YOU'RE A CLOWN, AND THESE ARE PIES.
DO WHAT YOU MUST.

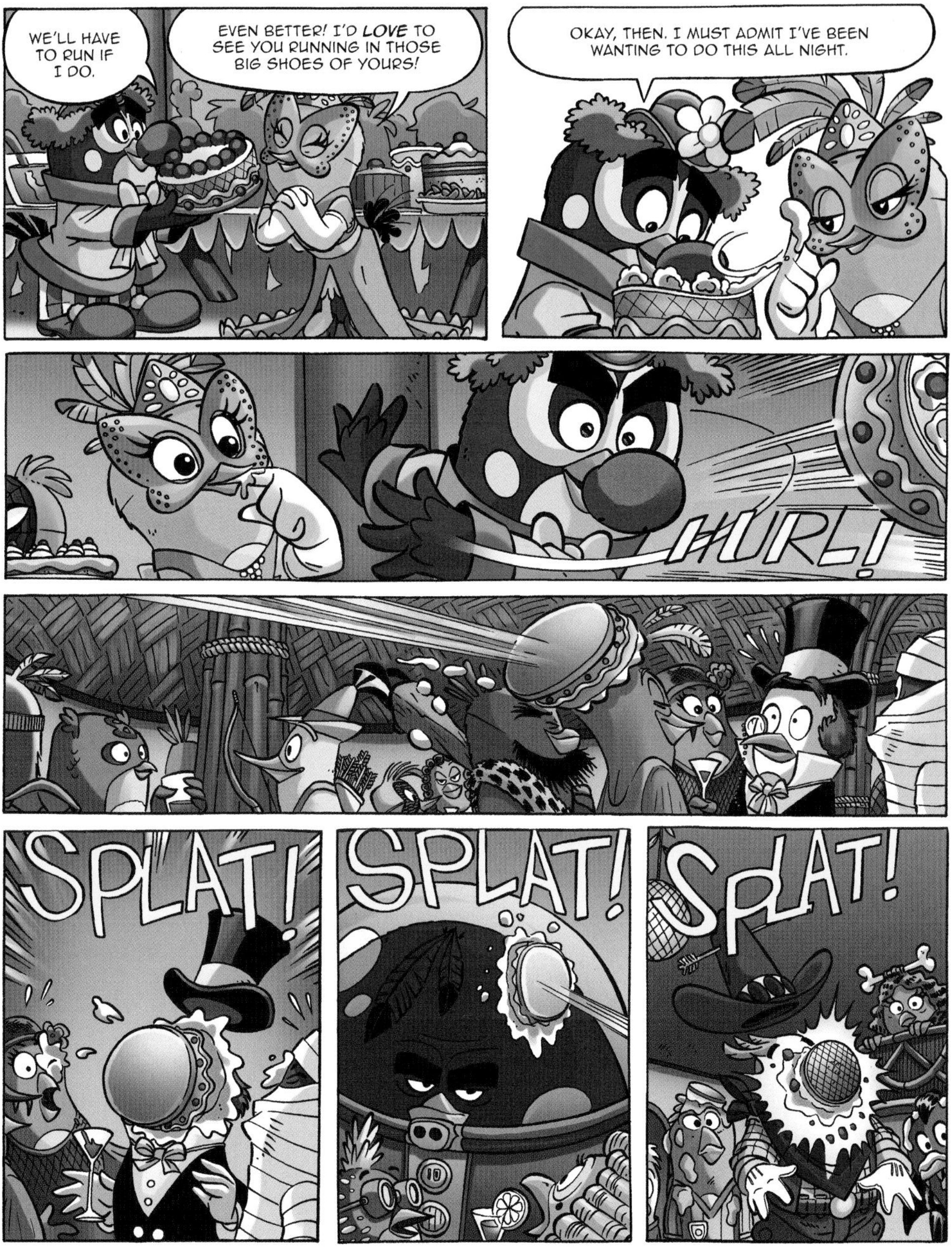

WE'LL HAVE TO RUN IF I DO.
EVEN BETTER! I'D LOVE TO SEE YOU RUNNING IN THOSE BIG SHOES OF YOURS!
OKAY, THEN. I MUST ADMIT I'VE BEEN WANTING TO DO THIS ALL NIGHT.
HURL!
SPLAT!
SPLAT!
SPLAT!

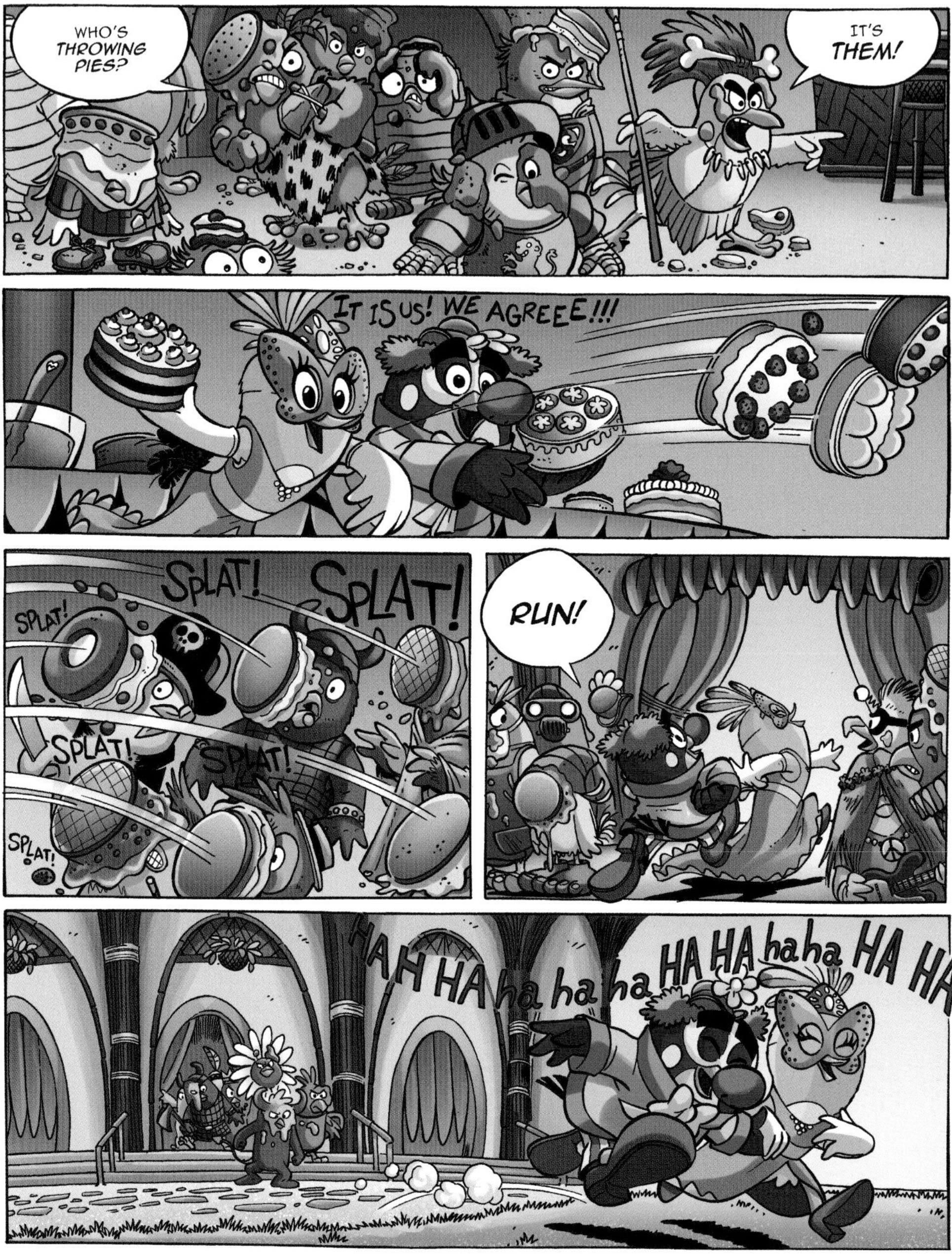
WHO'S THROWING PIES?
IT'S THEM!
IT IS US! WE AGREEE!!!
SPLAT!
SPLAT!
SPLAT!
SPLAT!
SPLAT!
SPLAT!
RUN!
HAH HA ha ha ha HA HA haha HA HA

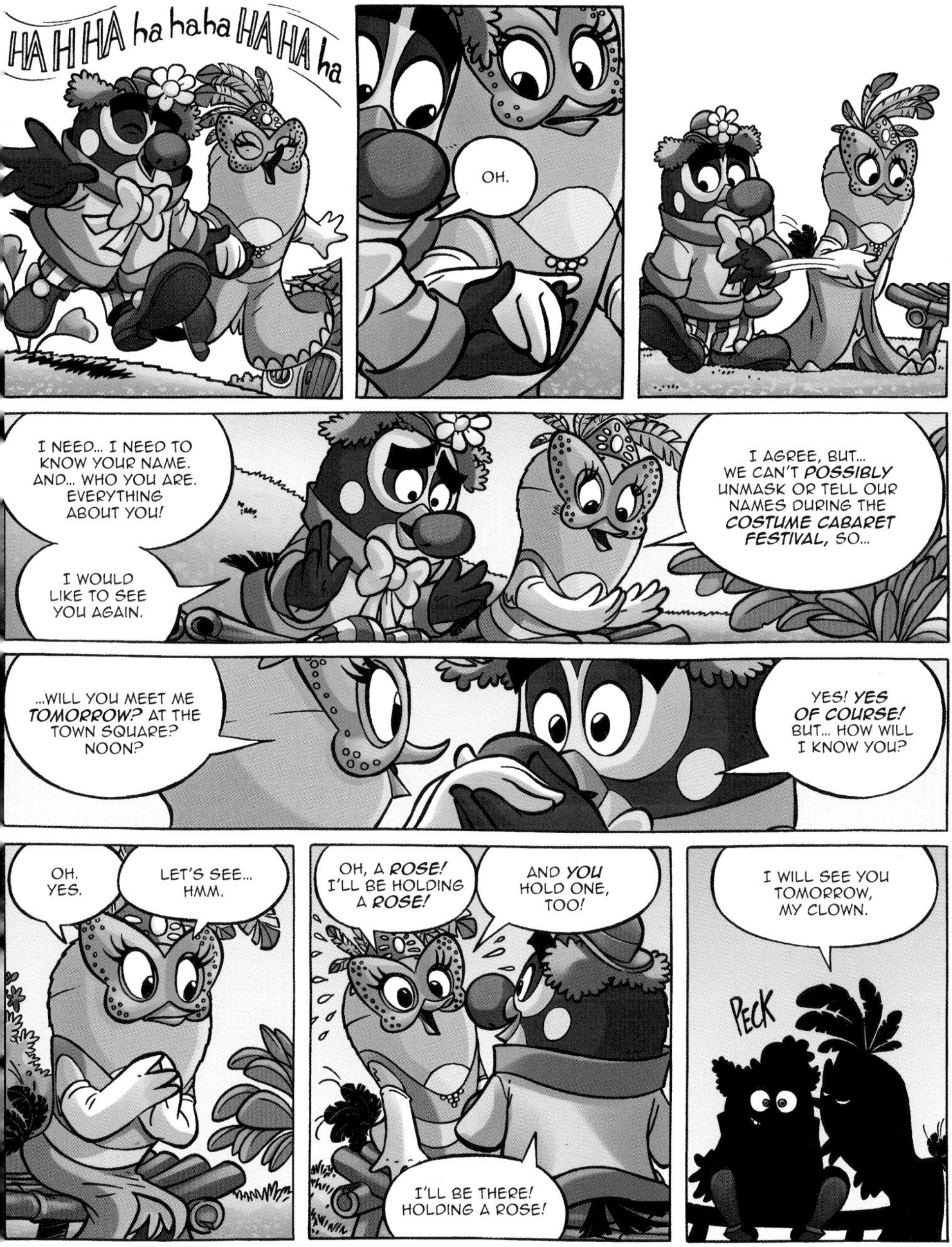
HA H HA ha ha ha HA HA ha
OH.
I NEED... I NEED TO KNOW YOUR NAME. AND... WHO YOU ARE. EVERYTHING ABOUT YOU!
I WOULD LIKE TO SEE YOU AGAIN.
I AGREE, BUT... WE CAN'T *POSSIBLY* UNMASK OR TELL OUR NAMES DURING THE ***COSTUME CABARET FESTIVAL,*** SO...
...WILL YOU MEET ME *TOMORROW?* AT THE TOWN SQUARE? NOON?
YES! *YES OF COURSE!* BUT... HOW WILL I KNOW YOU?
OH. YES.
LET'S SEE... HMM.
OH, A *ROSE!* I'LL BE HOLDING A *ROSE!*
AND *YOU* HOLD ONE, TOO!
I'LL BE THERE! HOLDING A ROSE!
I WILL SEE YOU TOMORROW, MY CLOWN.
PECK

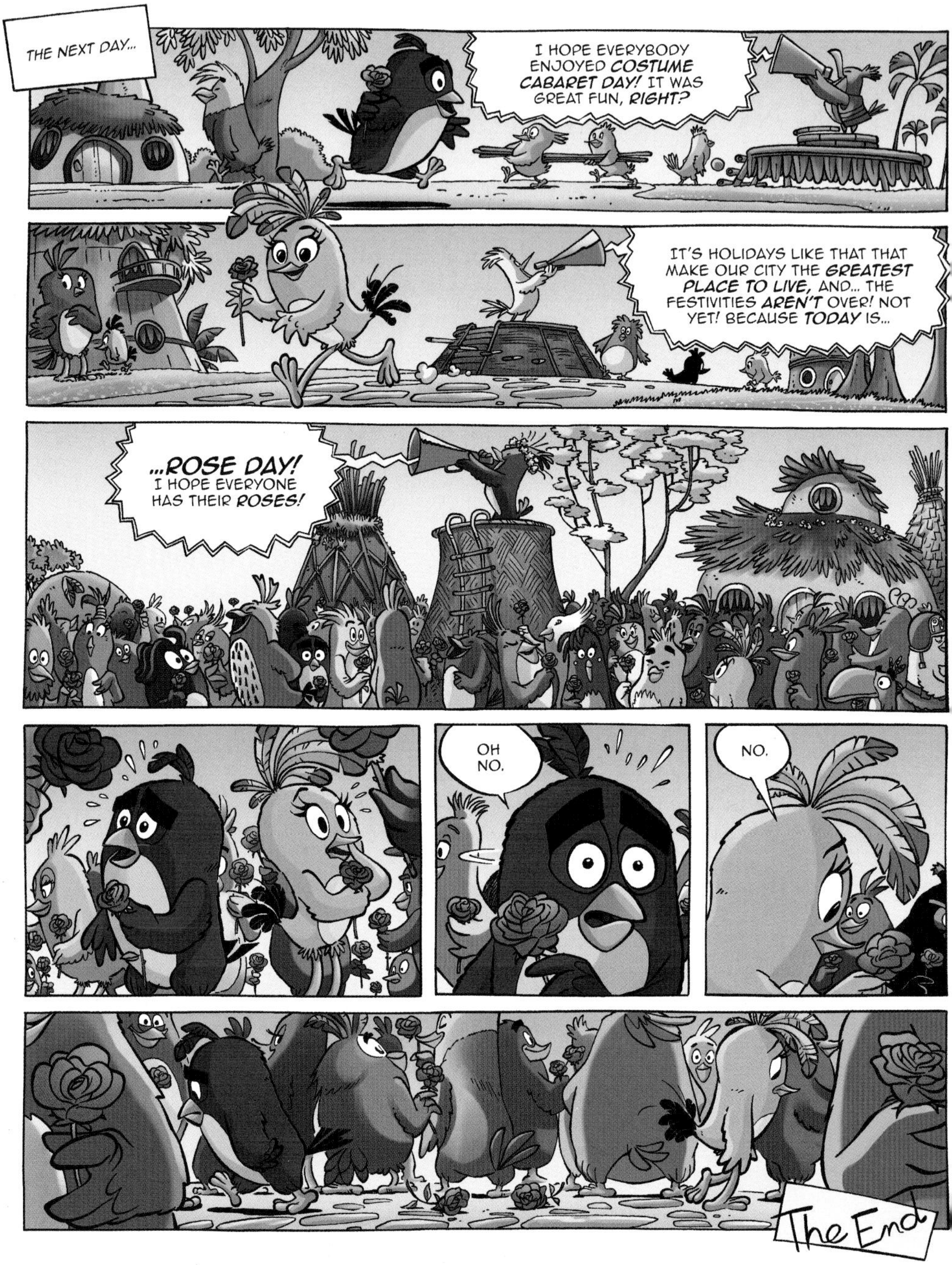
THE NEXT DAY...
I HOPE EVERYBODY ENJOYED COSTUME CABARET DAY! IT WAS GREAT FUN, RIGHT?
IT'S HOLIDAYS LIKE THAT THAT MAKE OUR CITY THE GREATEST PLACE TO LIVE, AND... THE FESTIVITIES AREN'T OVER! NOT YET! BECAUSE TODAY IS...
...ROSE DAY! I HOPE EVERYONE HAS THEIR ROSES!
OH NO.
NO.
The End

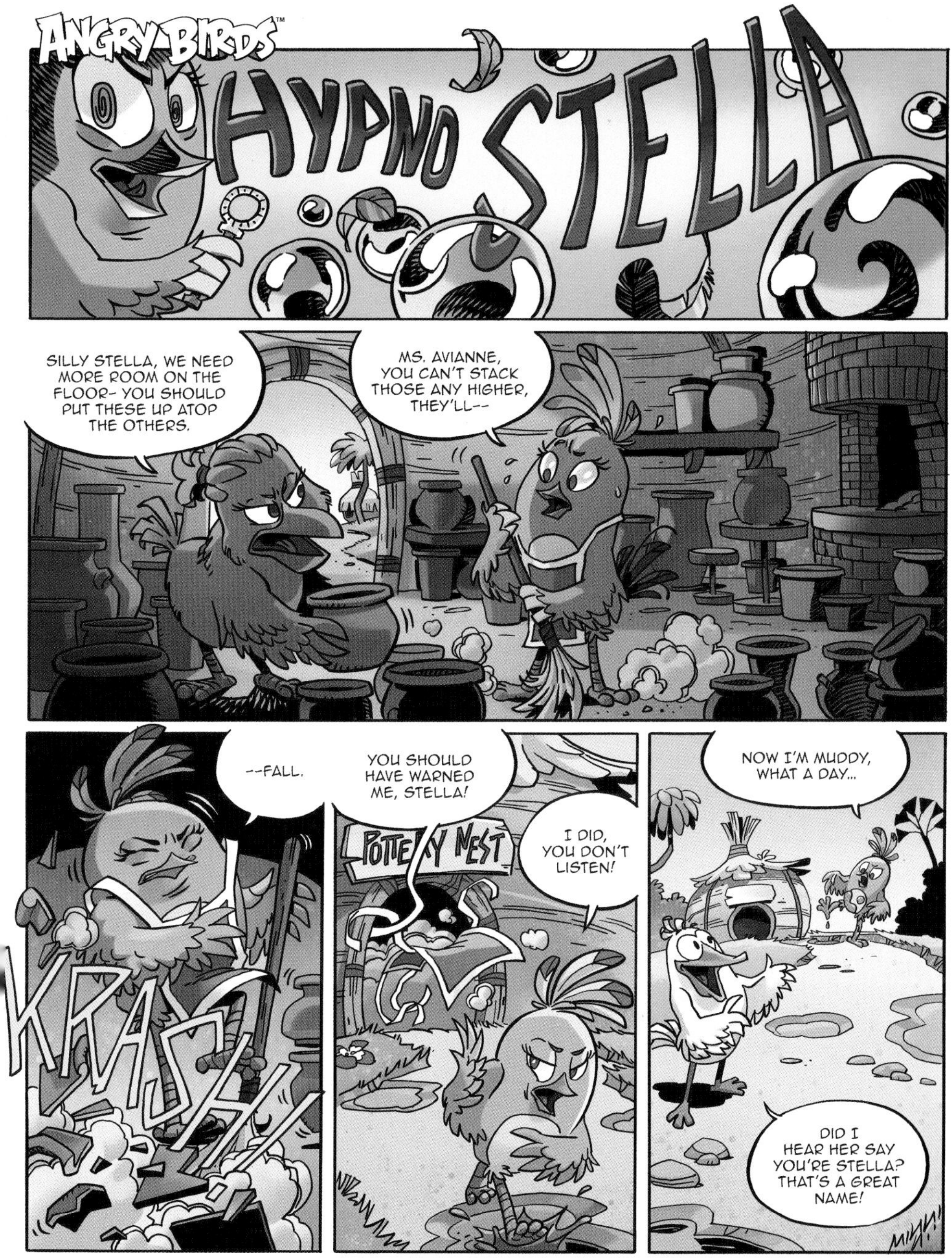
ANGRY BIRDS
HYPNO STELLA
SILLY STELLA, WE NEED MORE ROOM ON THE FLOOR- YOU SHOULD PUT THESE UP ATOP THE OTHERS.
MS. AVIANNE, YOU CAN'T STACK THOSE ANY HIGHER, THEY'LL--
--FALL.
KRASH!!
YOU SHOULD HAVE WARNED ME, STELLA!
POTTERY NEST
I DID, YOU DON'T LISTEN!
NOW I'M MUDDY, WHAT A DAY...
DID I HEAR HER SAY YOU'RE STELLA? THAT'S A GREAT NAME!

SCRIPT BY **JEFF PARKER** • ART & INKS BY **JEAN-MICHEL BOESCH** • COLORS BY **NICOLA PASQUETTO**

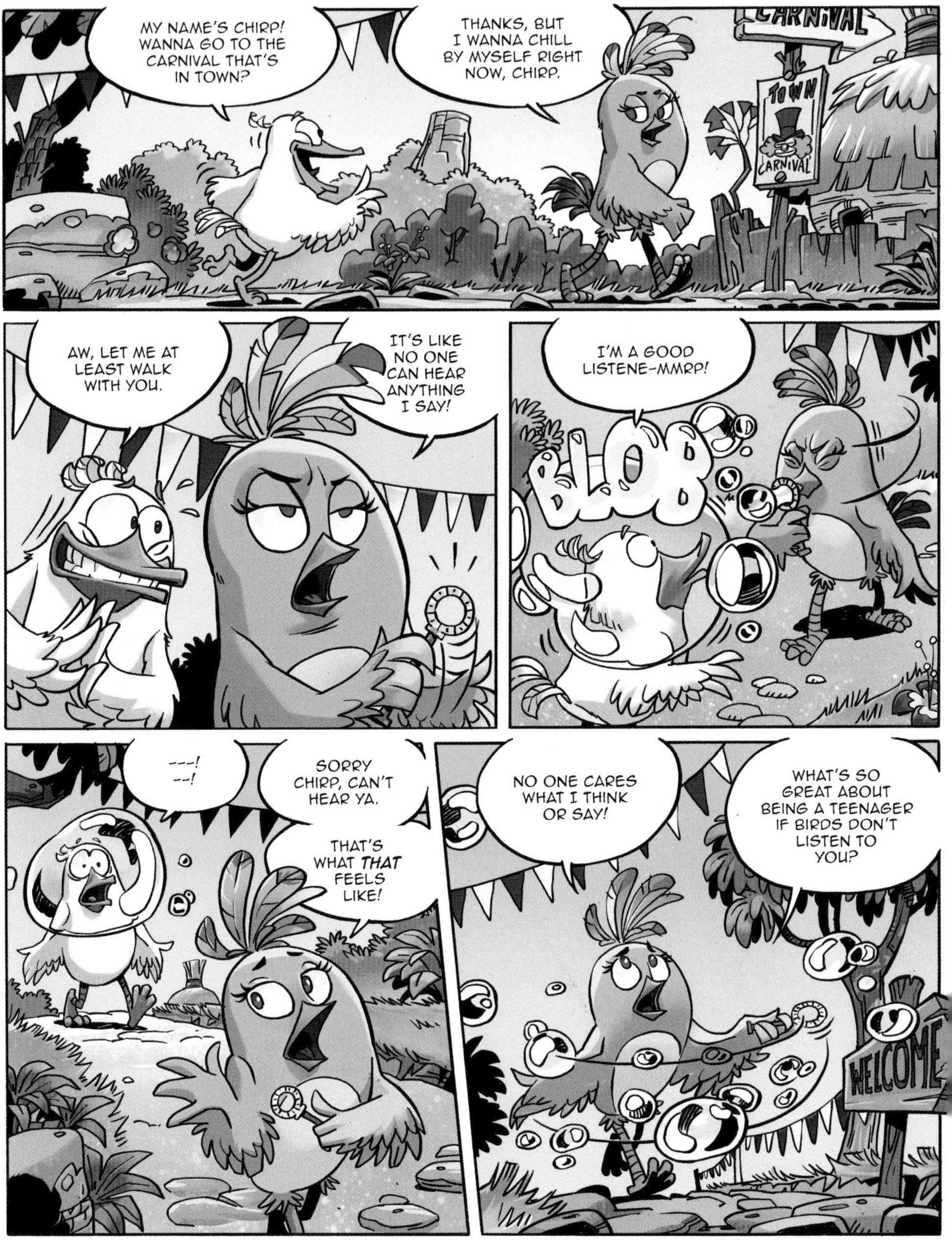
MY NAME'S CHIRP! WANNA GO TO THE CARNIVAL THAT'S IN TOWN?
THANKS, BUT I WANNA CHILL BY MYSELF RIGHT NOW, CHIRP.
CARNIVAL
TOWN
CARNIVAL
AW, LET ME AT LEAST WALK WITH YOU.
IT'S LIKE NO ONE CAN HEAR ANYTHING I SAY!
I'M A GOOD LISTENE-MMRP!
BLOB
---! --!
SORRY CHIRP, CAN'T HEAR YA.
THAT'S WHAT *THAT* FEELS LIKE!
NO ONE CARES WHAT I THINK OR SAY!
WHAT'S SO GREAT ABOUT BEING A TEENAGER IF BIRDS DON'T LISTEN TO YOU?
WELCOME

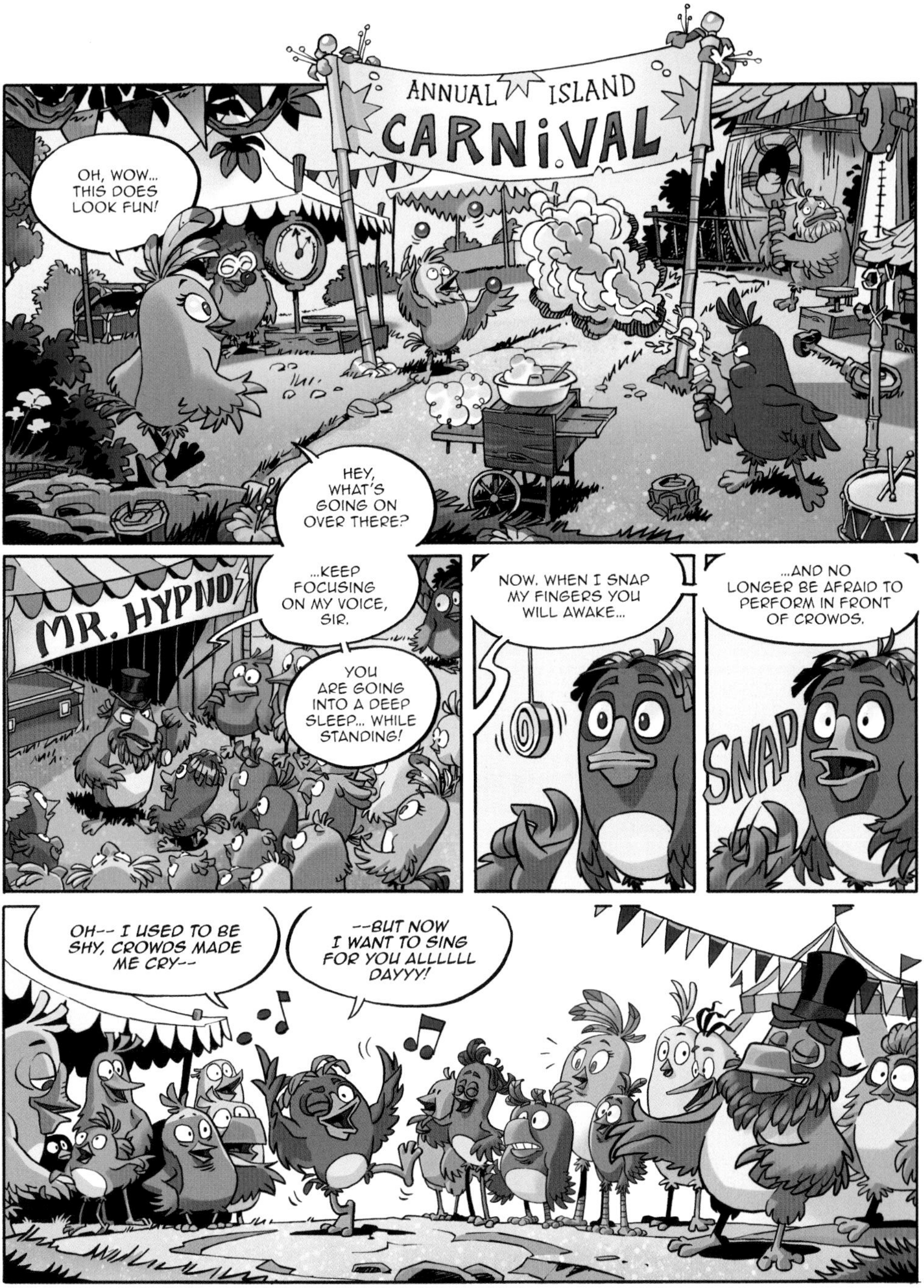

ANNUAL ISLAND CARNiVAL
OH, WOW... THIS DOES LOOK FUN!
HEY, WHAT'S GOING ON OVER THERE?
MR. HYPNO
...KEEP FOCUSING ON MY VOICE, SIR.
YOU ARE GOING INTO A DEEP SLEEP... WHILE STANDING!
NOW. WHEN I SNAP MY FINGERS YOU WILL AWAKE...
...AND NO LONGER BE AFRAID TO PERFORM IN FRONT OF CROWDS.
SNAP
OH-- I USED TO BE SHY, CROWDS MADE ME CRY--
--BUT NOW I WANT TO SING FOR YOU ALLLLLL DAYYY!

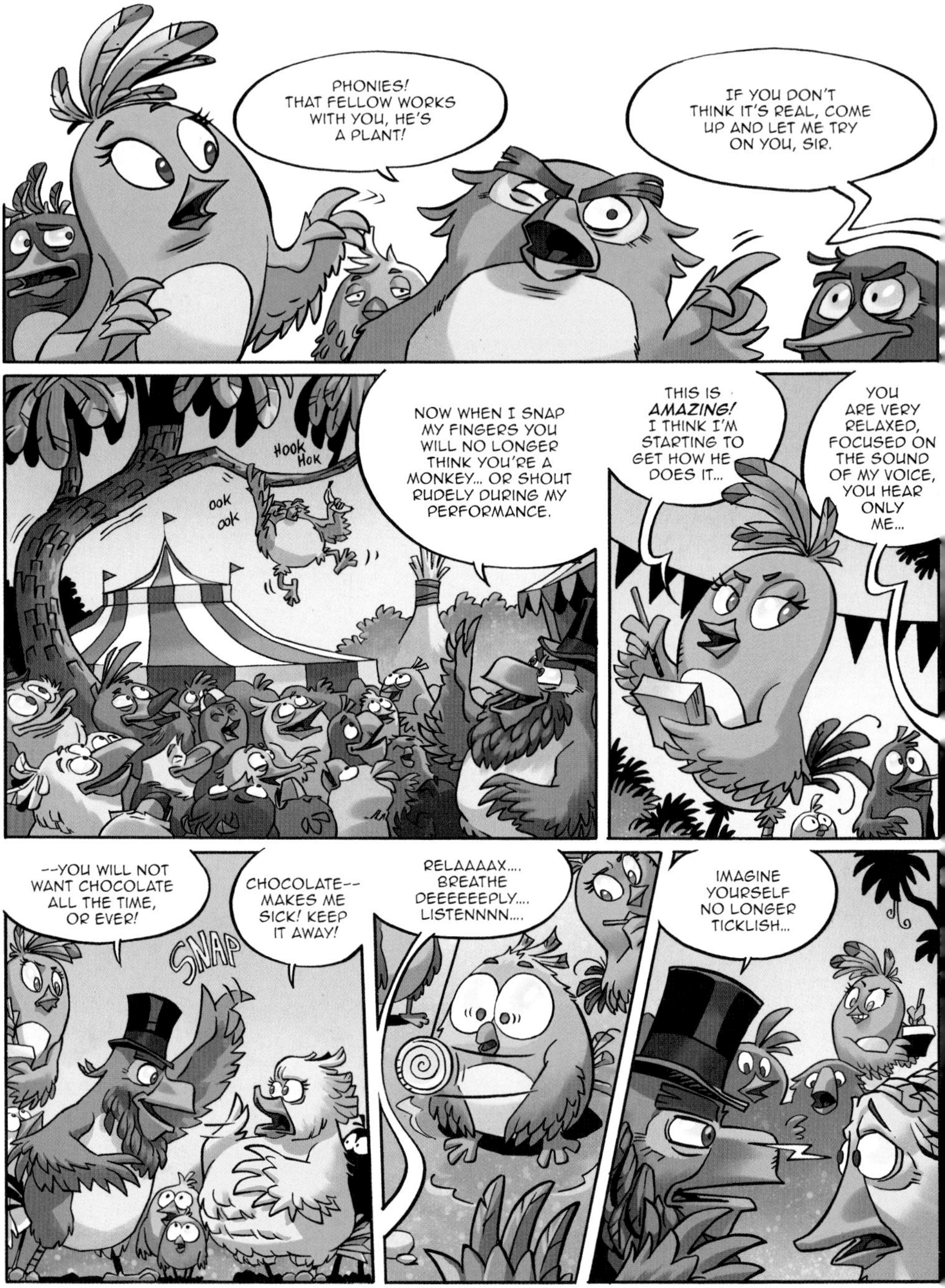
PHONIES! THAT FELLOW WORKS WITH YOU, HE'S A PLANT!
IF YOU DON'T THINK IT'S REAL, COME UP AND LET ME TRY ON YOU, SIR.
HOOK HOK
OOK OOK
NOW WHEN I SNAP MY FINGERS YOU WILL NO LONGER THINK YOU'RE A MONKEY... OR SHOUT RUDELY DURING MY PERFORMANCE.
THIS IS *AMAZING!* I THINK I'M STARTING TO GET HOW HE DOES IT...
YOU ARE VERY RELAXED, FOCUSED ON THE SOUND OF MY VOICE, YOU HEAR ONLY ME...
--YOU WILL NOT WANT CHOCOLATE ALL THE TIME, OR EVER!
SNAP
CHOCOLATE--MAKES ME SICK! KEEP IT AWAY!
RELAAAAX.... BREATHE DEEEEEEPLY.... LISTENNNN....
IMAGINE YOURSELF NO LONGER TICKLISH...

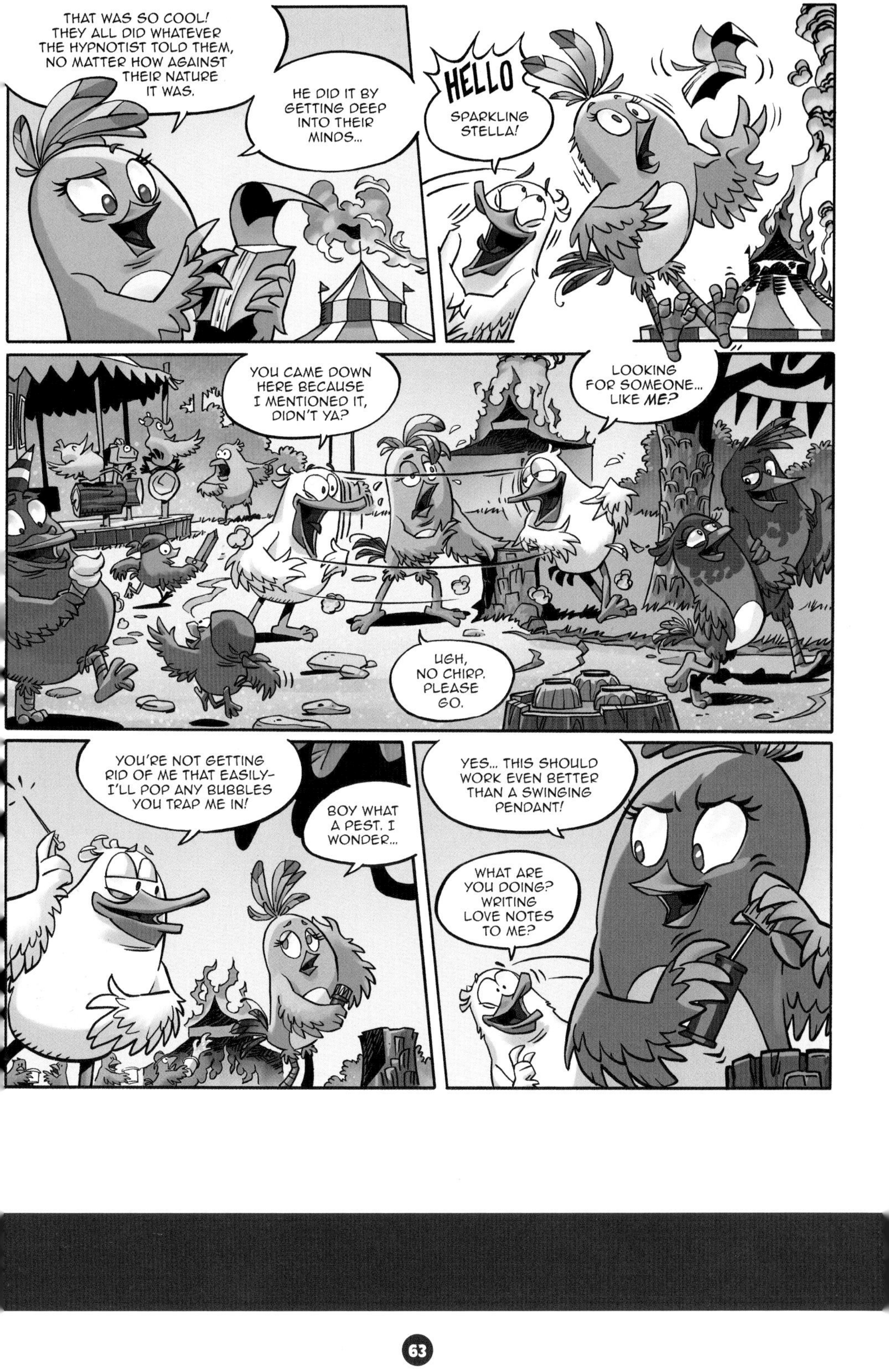

THAT WAS SO COOL! THEY ALL DID WHATEVER THE HYPNOTIST TOLD THEM, NO MATTER HOW AGAINST THEIR NATURE IT WAS.
HE DID IT BY GETTING DEEP INTO THEIR MINDS...
HELLO
SPARKLING STELLA!
YOU CAME DOWN HERE BECAUSE I MENTIONED IT, DIDN'T YA?
LOOKING FOR SOMEONE... LIKE ME?
UGH, NO CHIRP. PLEASE GO.
YOU'RE NOT GETTING RID OF ME THAT EASILY- I'LL POP ANY BUBBLES YOU TRAP ME IN!
BOY WHAT A PEST. I WONDER...
YES... THIS SHOULD WORK EVEN BETTER THAN A SWINGING PENDANT!
WHAT ARE YOU DOING? WRITING LOVE NOTES TO ME?

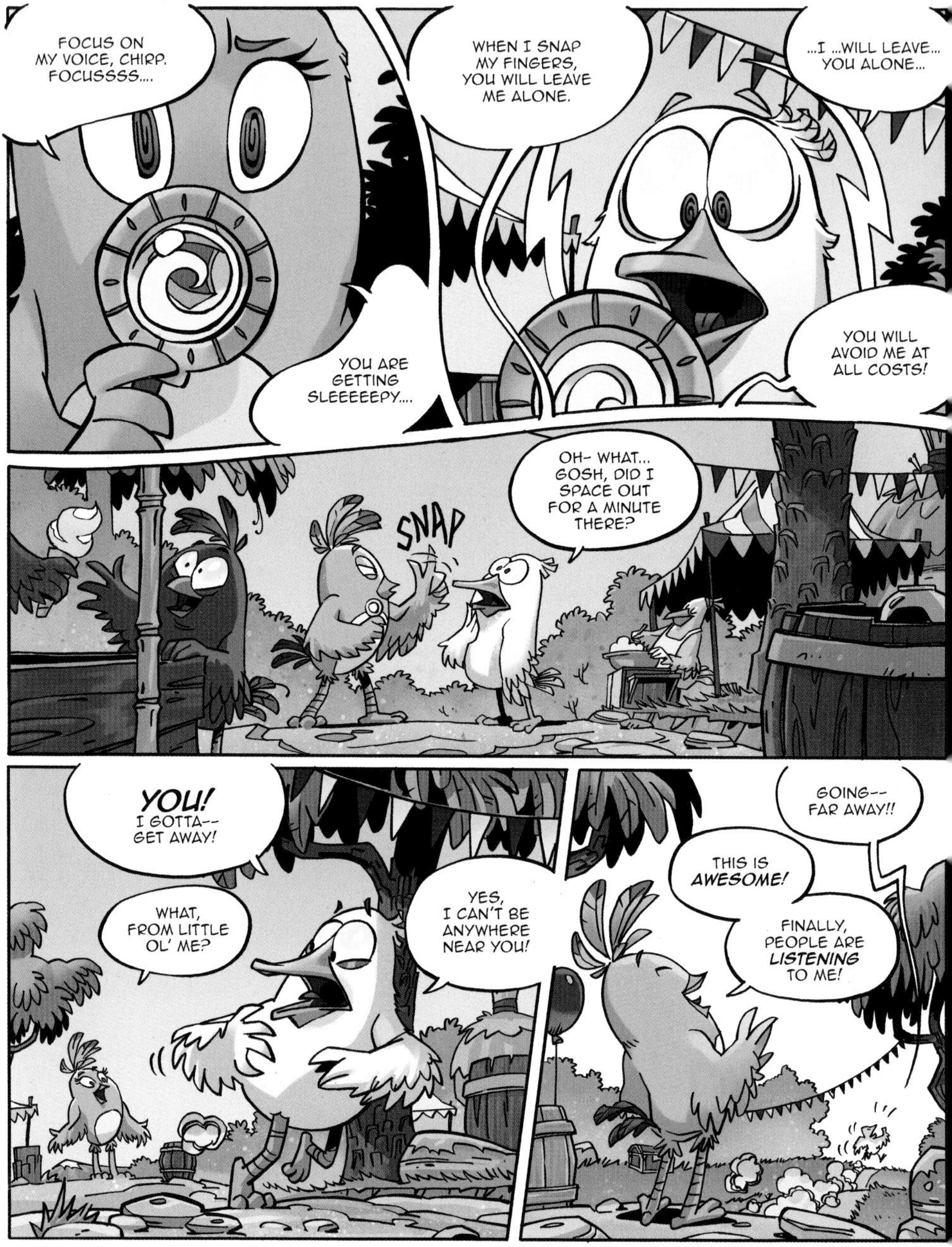
FOCUS ON MY VOICE, CHIRP. FOCUSSSS....
YOU ARE GETTING SLEEEEEPY....
WHEN I SNAP MY FINGERS, YOU WILL LEAVE ME ALONE.
...I ...WILL LEAVE... YOU ALONE...
YOU WILL AVOID ME AT ALL COSTS!
SNAP
OH- WHAT... GOSH, DID I SPACE OUT FOR A MINUTE THERE?
YOU! I GOTTA-- GET AWAY!
WHAT, FROM LITTLE OL' ME?
YES, I CAN'T BE ANYWHERE NEAR YOU!
GOING-- FAR AWAY!!
THIS IS AWESOME!
FINALLY, PEOPLE ARE LISTENING TO ME!

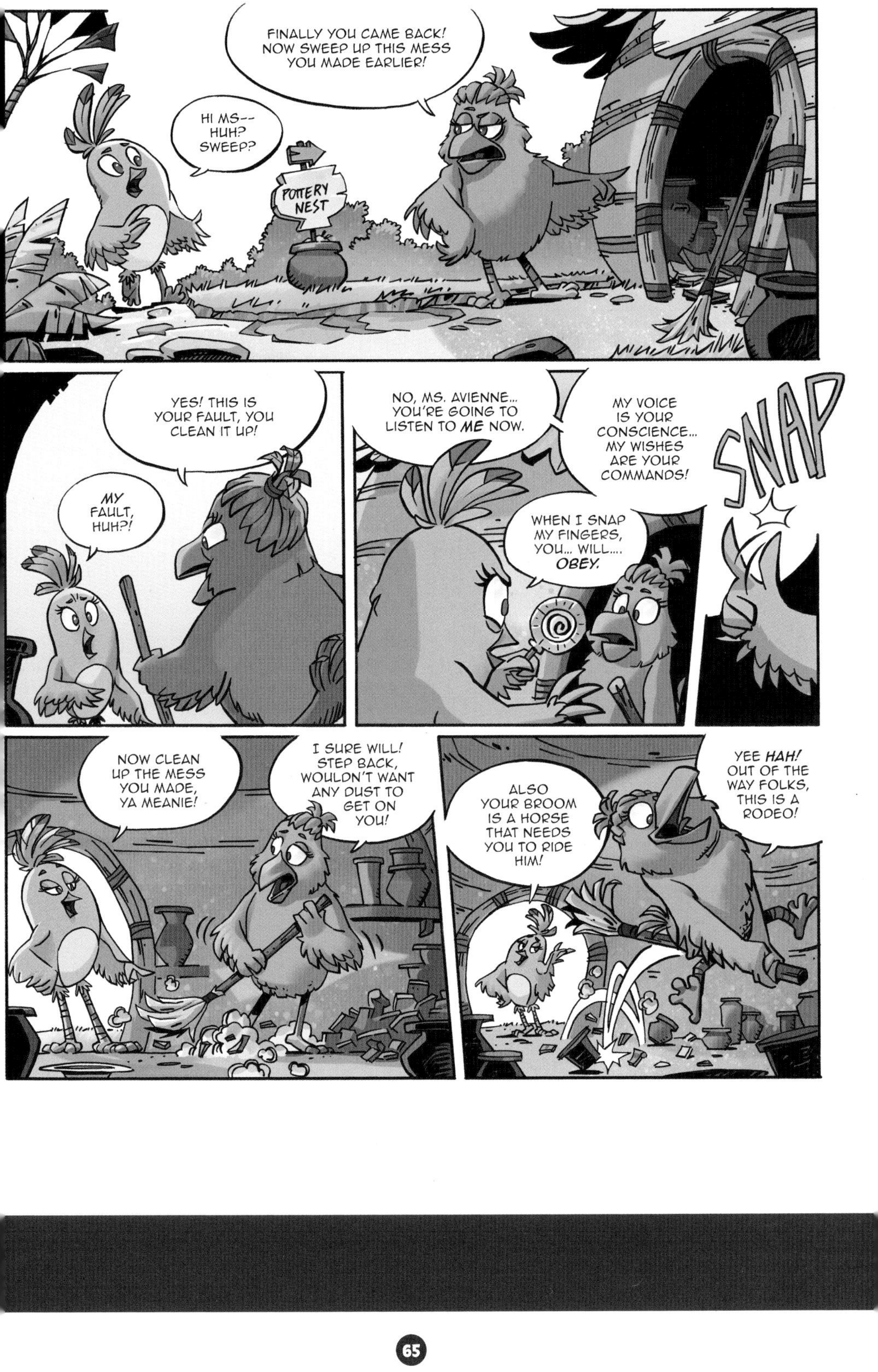

FINALLY YOU CAME BACK! NOW SWEEP UP THIS MESS YOU MADE EARLIER!
HI MS-- HUH? SWEEP?
POTTERY NEST
YES! THIS IS YOUR FAULT, YOU CLEAN IT UP!
MY FAULT, HUH?!
NO, MS. AVIENNE... YOU'RE GOING TO LISTEN TO ME NOW.
MY VOICE IS YOUR CONSCIENCE... MY WISHES ARE YOUR COMMANDS!
WHEN I SNAP MY FINGERS, YOU... WILL.... OBEY.
SNAP
NOW CLEAN UP THE MESS YOU MADE, YA MEANIE!
I SURE WILL! STEP BACK, WOULDN'T WANT ANY DUST TO GET ON YOU!
ALSO YOUR BROOM IS A HORSE THAT NEEDS YOU TO RIDE HIM!
YEE HAH! OUT OF THE WAY FOLKS, THIS IS A RODEO!

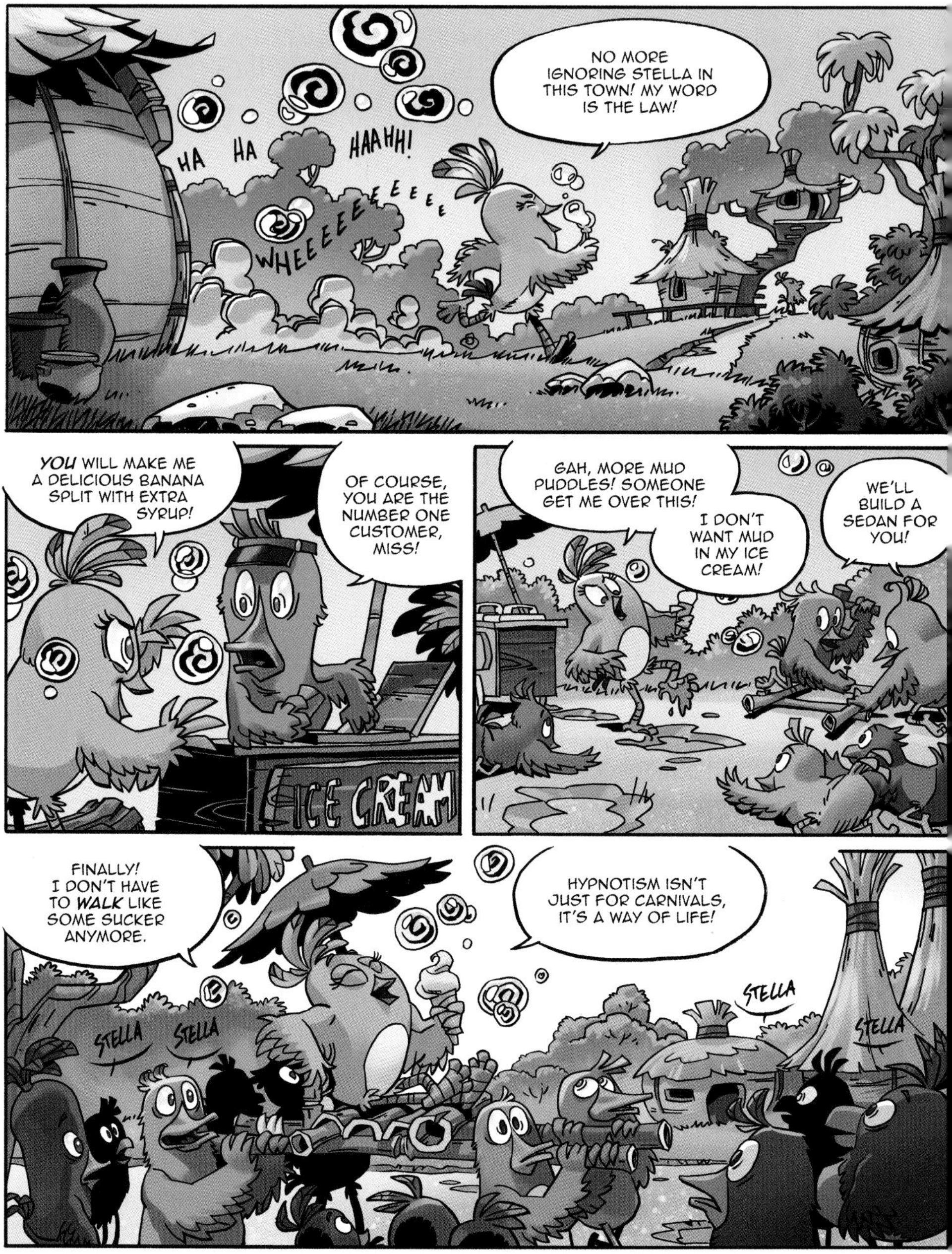
NO MORE IGNORING STELLA IN THIS TOWN! MY WORD IS THE LAW!
HA HA HAAHH!
WHEEEEEEEEEEE
YOU WILL MAKE ME A DELICIOUS BANANA SPLIT WITH EXTRA SYRUP!
OF COURSE, YOU ARE THE NUMBER ONE CUSTOMER, MISS!
ICE CREAM
GAH, MORE MUD PUDDLES! SOMEONE GET ME OVER THIS!
I DON'T WANT MUD IN MY ICE CREAM!
WE'LL BUILD A SEDAN FOR YOU!
FINALLY! I DON'T HAVE TO WALK LIKE SOME SUCKER ANYMORE.
HYPNOTISM ISN'T JUST FOR CARNIVALS, IT'S A WAY OF LIFE!
STELLA
STELLA
STELLA
STELLA

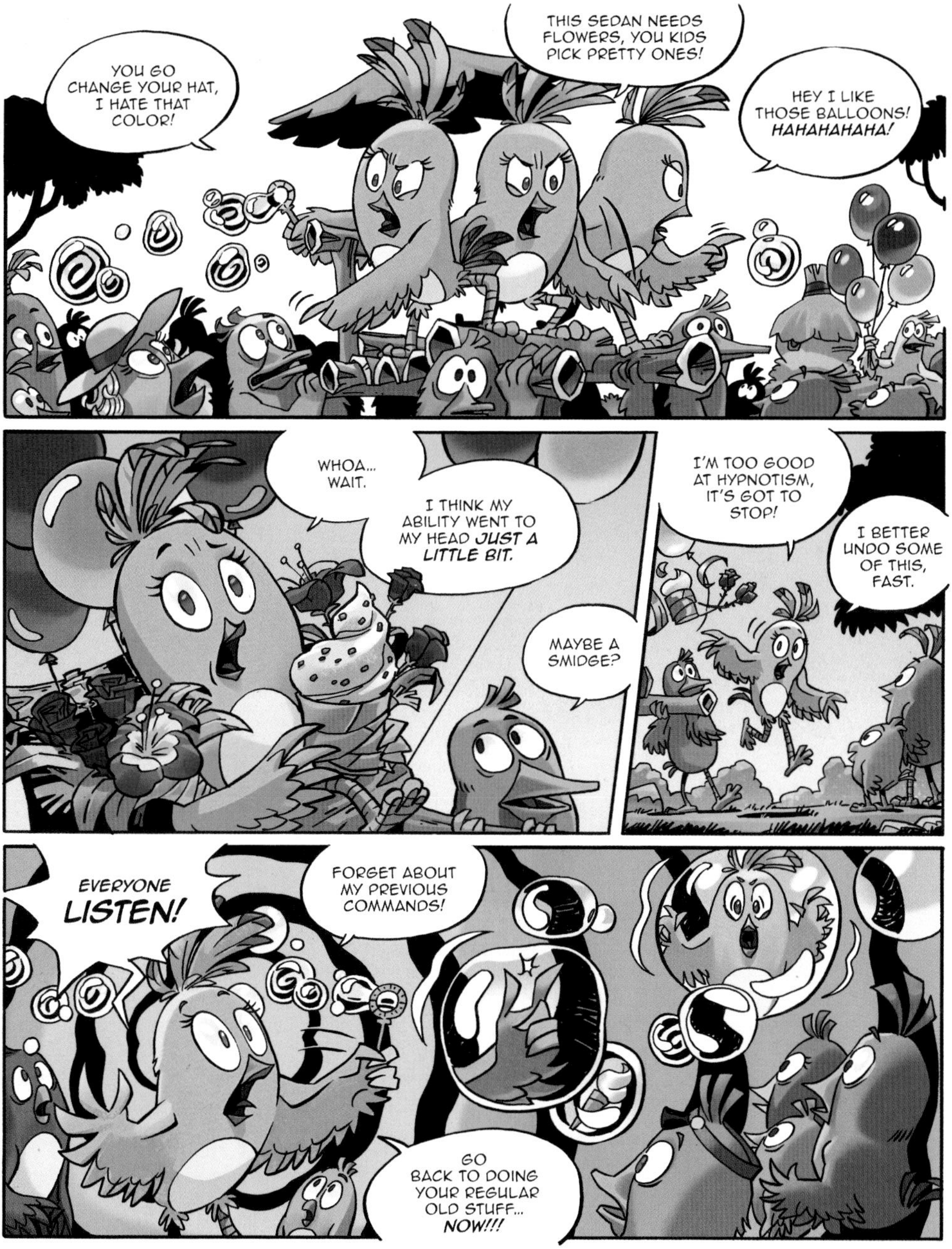
YOU GO CHANGE YOUR HAT, I HATE THAT COLOR!
THIS SEDAN NEEDS FLOWERS, YOU KIDS PICK PRETTY ONES!
HEY I LIKE THOSE BALLOONS! HAHAHAHAHA!
WHOA... WAIT.
I THINK MY ABILITY WENT TO MY HEAD JUST A LITTLE BIT.
MAYBE A SMIDGE?
I'M TOO GOOD AT HYPNOTISM, IT'S GOT TO STOP!
I BETTER UNDO SOME OF THIS, FAST.
EVERYONE LISTEN!
FORGET ABOUT MY PREVIOUS COMMANDS!
GO BACK TO DOING YOUR REGULAR OLD STUFF... NOW!!!

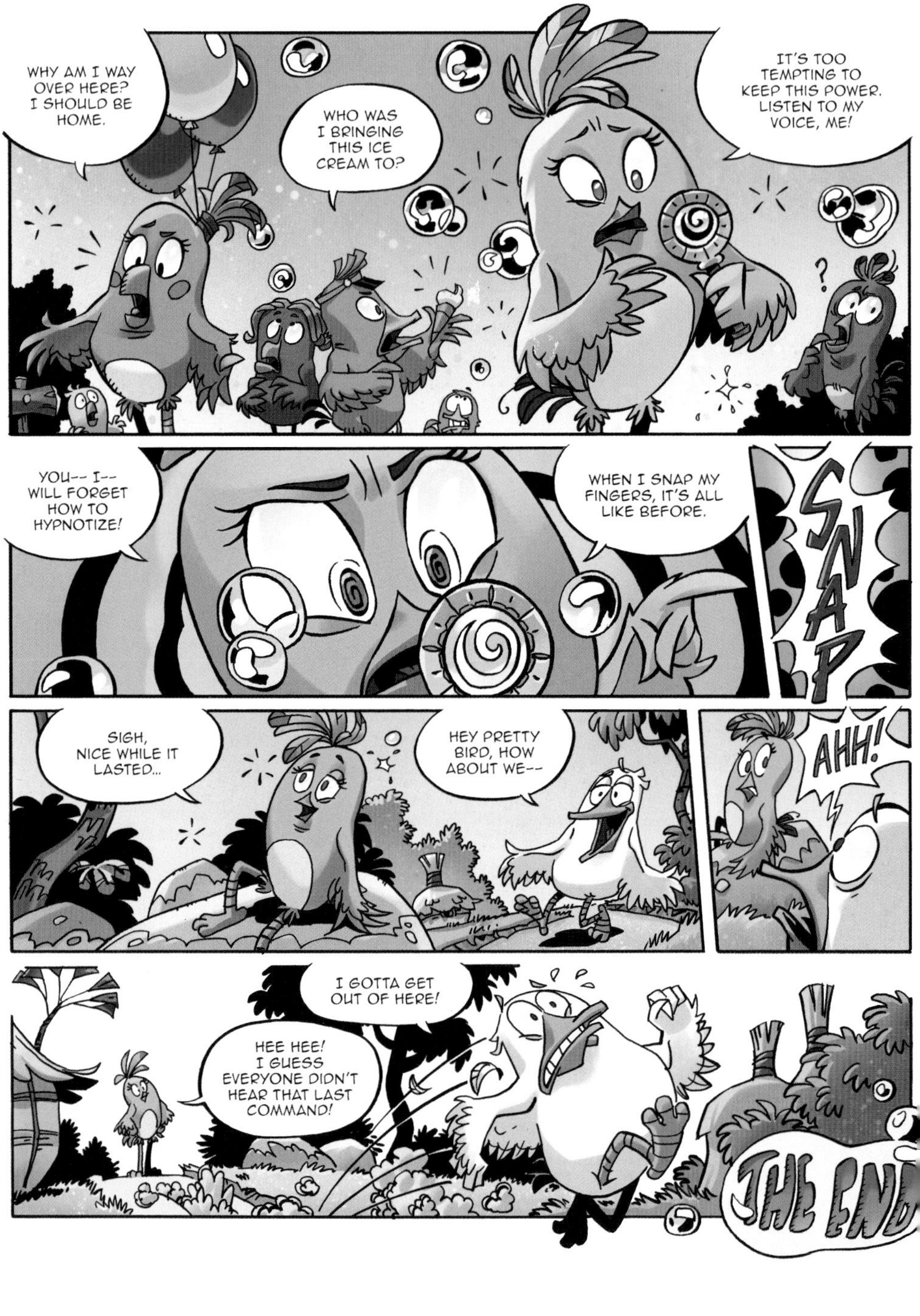

WHY AM I WAY OVER HERE? I SHOULD BE HOME.
WHO WAS I BRINGING THIS ICE CREAM TO?
IT'S TOO TEMPTING TO KEEP THIS POWER. LISTEN TO MY VOICE, ME!
YOU-- I-- WILL FORGET HOW TO HYPNOTIZE!
WHEN I SNAP MY FINGERS, IT'S ALL LIKE BEFORE.
SNAP
SIGH, NICE WHILE IT LASTED...
HEY PRETTY BIRD, HOW ABOUT WE--
AHH!
I GOTTA GET OUT OF HERE!
HEE HEE! I GUESS EVERYONE DIDN'T HEAR THAT LAST COMMAND!
THE END

RED IN THE BIRD
NHO CRIED
WOLF
ANGRY BIRDS
GOBBLE GAZETTE IS... NOW HIRING! BE A NEWSPAPER REPORTER! GOOD PAY! EXCITING WORK!
SO, YOU WANT TO BE A NEWSPAPER REPORTER, HUH? WELL, THIS JOB IS ALL ABOUT EXCITEMENT, SO...
...SAY SOMETHING EXCITING!
UHH...?
WATERMELON EXPLOSION?
WATERMELON EXPLOSION?
I LIKE THAT!
YOU'RE HIRED.
HERE'S A TYPEWRITER.
HERE'S A TIE.
OOF!
NOW GET TO WORK!

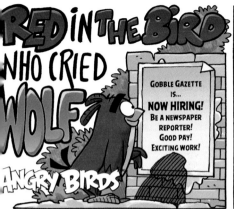

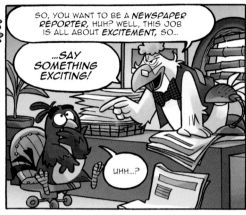

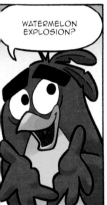

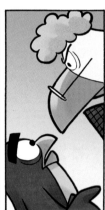

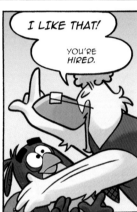

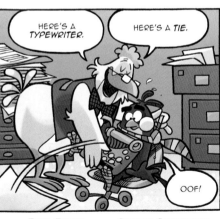

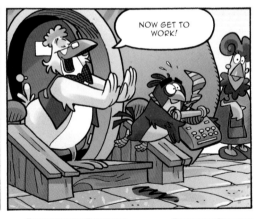

RIPT BY **PAUL TOBIN** • ART BY **GIORGIO CAVAZZANO** • INKS BY **ALESSANDRO ZEMOLIN** • COLORS BY **DIGIKORE STUDIOS**

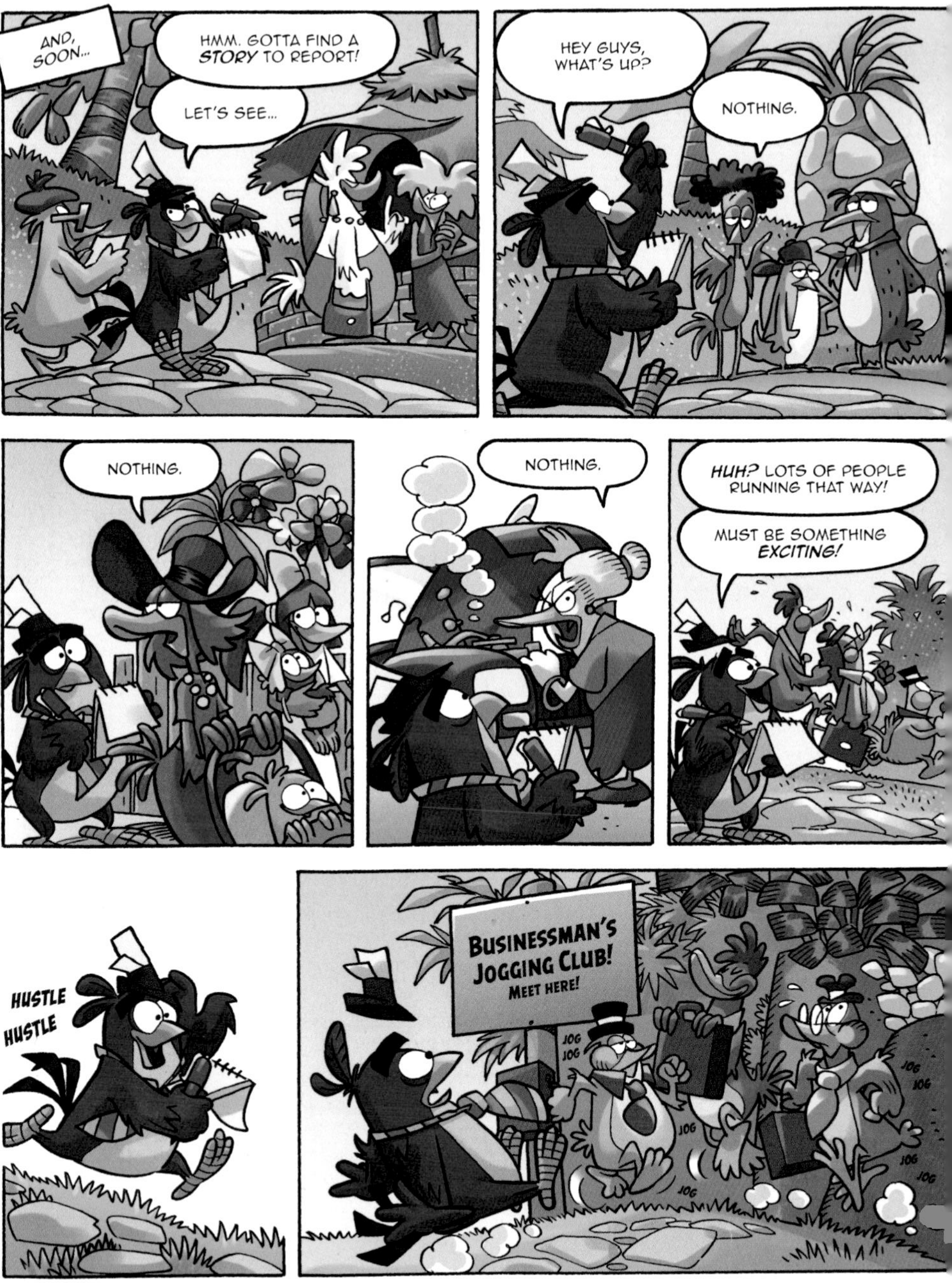
AND, SOON...
HMM. GOTTA FIND A STORY TO REPORT!
LET'S SEE...
HEY GUYS, WHAT'S UP?
NOTHING.
NOTHING.
NOTHING.
HUH? LOTS OF PEOPLE RUNNING THAT WAY!
MUST BE SOMETHING EXCITING!
HUSTLE HUSTLE
BUSINESSMAN'S JOGGING CLUB! MEET HERE!
JOG JOG
JOG
JOG
JOG JOG
JOG JOG

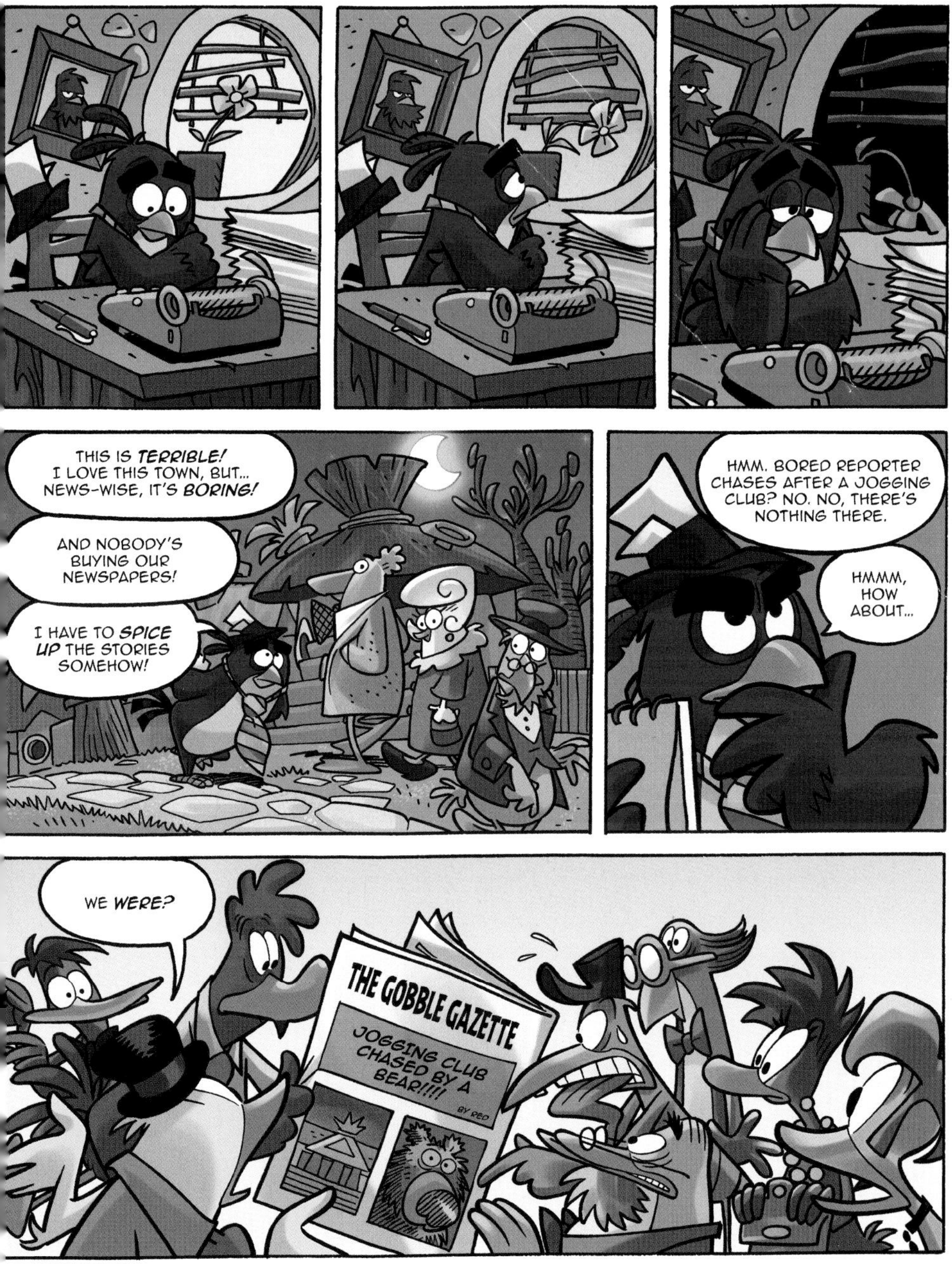
THIS IS TERRIBLE! I LOVE THIS TOWN, BUT... NEWS-WISE, IT'S BORING!
AND NOBODY'S BUYING OUR NEWSPAPERS!
I HAVE TO SPICE UP THE STORIES SOMEHOW!
HMM. BORED REPORTER CHASES AFTER A JOGGING CLUB? NO. NO, THERE'S NOTHING THERE.
HMMM, HOW ABOUT...
WE WERE?
THE GOBBLE GAZETTE
JOGGING CLUB CHASED BY A BEAR!!!!
BY RED

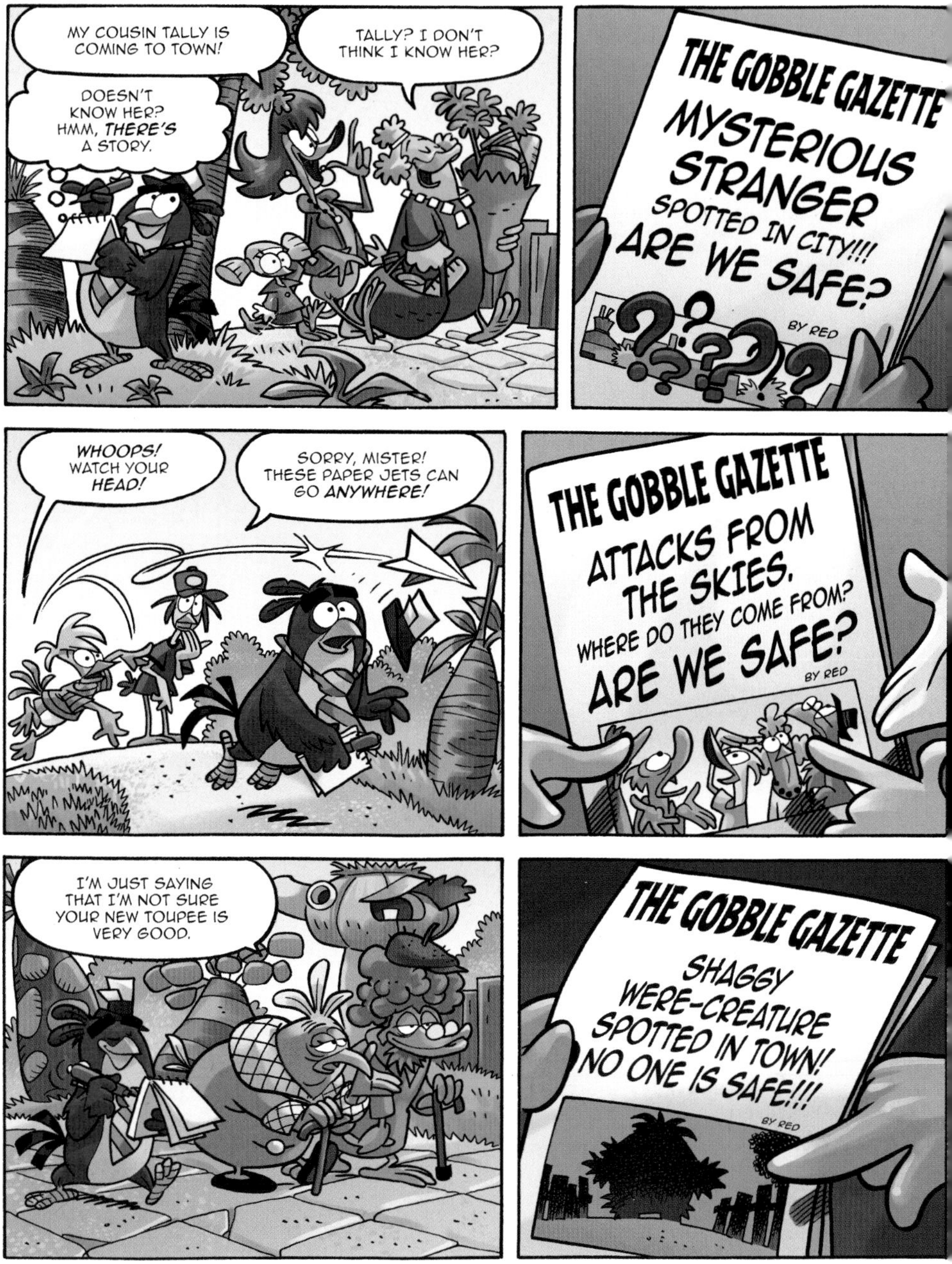
MY COUSIN TALLY IS COMING TO TOWN!
TALLY? I DON'T THINK I KNOW HER?
DOESN'T KNOW HER? HMM, THERE'S A STORY.
THE GOBBLE GAZETTE
MYSTERIOUS STRANGER SPOTTED IN CITY!!! ARE WE SAFE?
BY RED
WHOOPS! WATCH YOUR HEAD!
SORRY, MISTER! THESE PAPER JETS CAN GO ANYWHERE!
THE GOBBLE GAZETTE
ATTACKS FROM THE SKIES. WHERE DO THEY COME FROM? ARE WE SAFE?
BY RED
I'M JUST SAYING THAT I'M NOT SURE YOUR NEW TOUPEE IS VERY GOOD.
THE GOBBLE GAZETTE
SHAGGY WERE-CREATURE SPOTTED IN TOWN! NO ONE IS SAFE!!!
BY RED

THE GOBBLE GAZETTE
UFO SEEN ABOVE TOWN!
HMM. A UFO?
OOO. SOUNDS SCARY.
THE GOBBLE GAZETTE
EARTHQUAKE IMMINENT?
BY RED
AN EARTHQUAKE?
ARE WE SAFE?
GOBBLE GAZETTE
FISHBOWLS ON YOUR HEADS?
BY RED
FISHBOWLS?
THE WORLD'S GONE MAD!

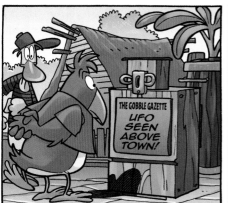

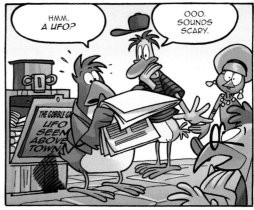

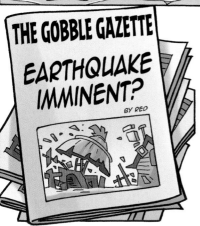

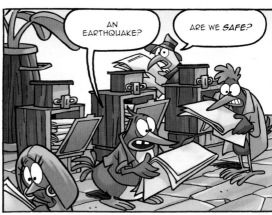

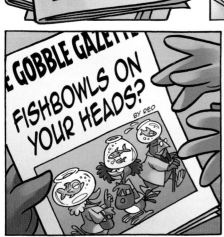

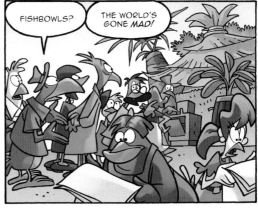

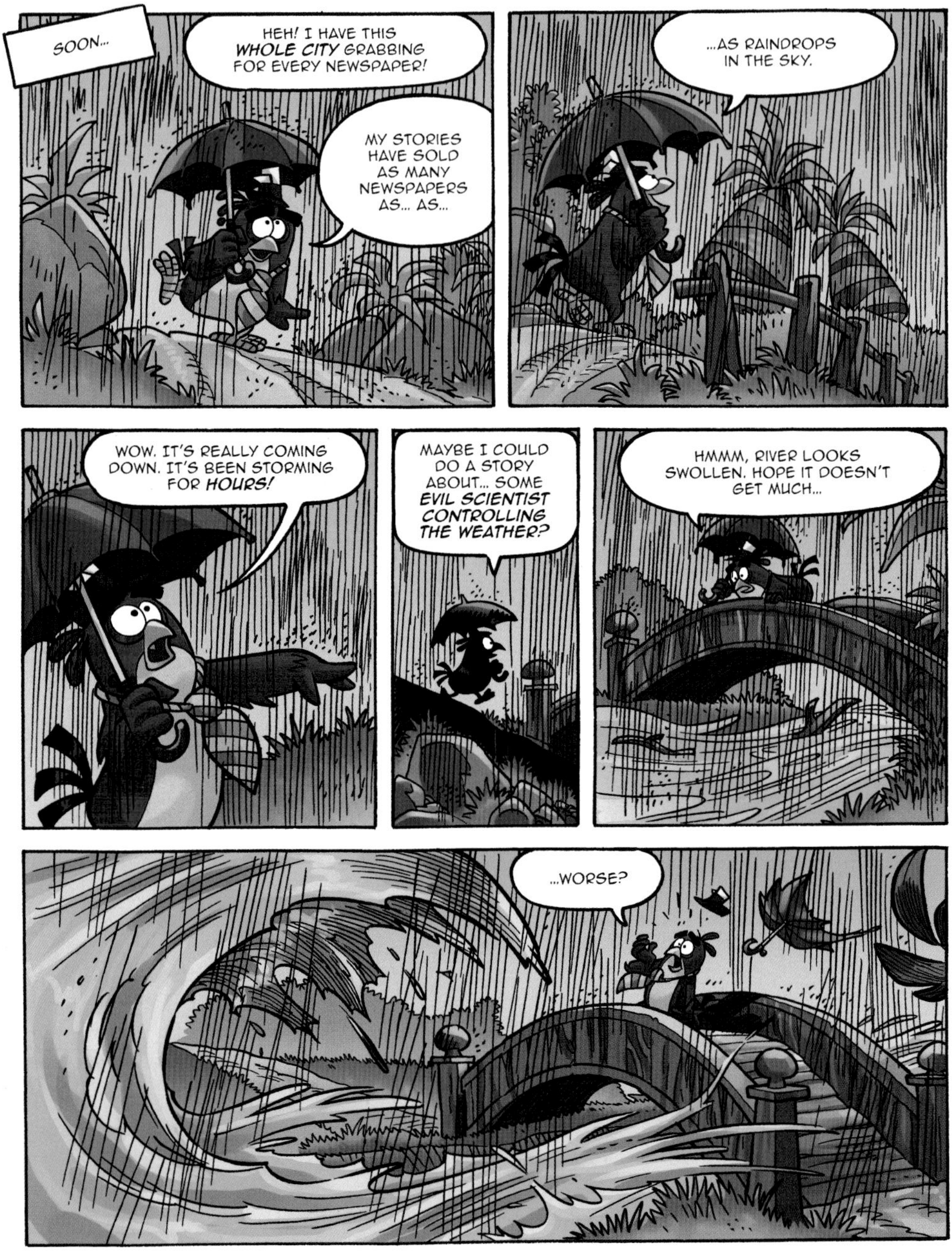
SOON...
HEH! I HAVE THIS WHOLE CITY GRABBING FOR EVERY NEWSPAPER!
MY STORIES HAVE SOLD AS MANY NEWSPAPERS AS... AS...
...AS RAINDROPS IN THE SKY.
WOW. IT'S REALLY COMING DOWN. IT'S BEEN STORMING FOR HOURS!
MAYBE I COULD DO A STORY ABOUT... SOME EVIL SCIENTIST CONTROLLING THE WEATHER?
HMMM, RIVER LOOKS SWOLLEN. HOPE IT DOESN'T GET MUCH...
...WORSE?

SOON...

FLASH FLOOD! FLASH FLOOD!

WE NEED SANDBAGS. PROTECT YOUR HOMES!

THERE'S A HUGE WALL OF WATER ON THE WAY!

LIKE WE'D BELIEVE *YOU.*

RIGHT. IT'S *OBVIOUSLY* MORE OF YOUR NONSENSE.

LISTEN, YOU RASCAL... THERE WERE *NO* UFOS. THERE *WASN'T* A SASQUATCH. THERE WERE NO HEROS OF *THREE-EYED VAMPIRE MOSQUITO BUFFALOS!*

OOF! OWW! OUCH!

WHY WON'T ANYONE BELIEVE ME BEFORE IT'S...

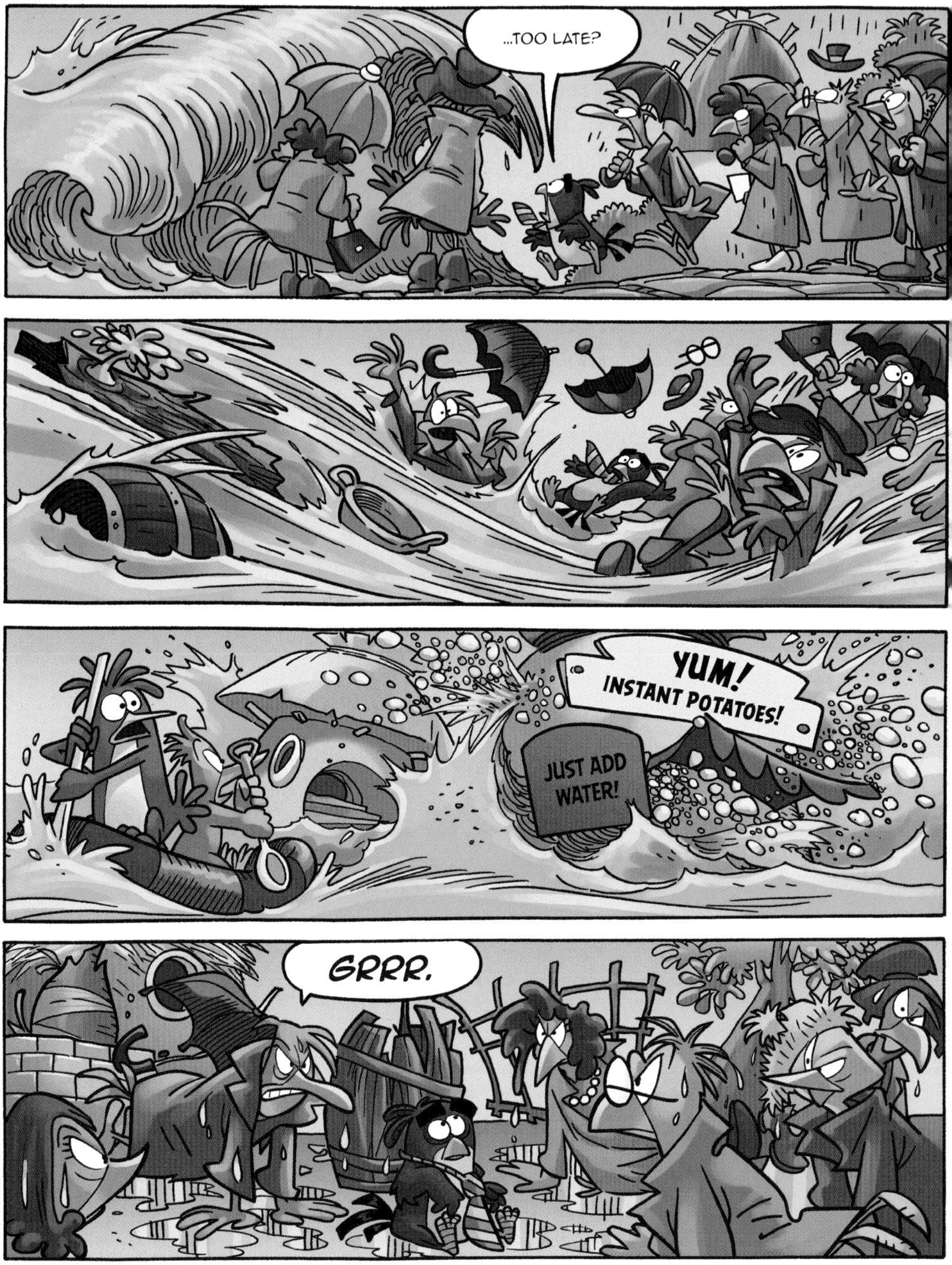
...TOO LATE?
YUM!
INSTANT POTATOES!
JUST ADD
WATER!
GRRR.

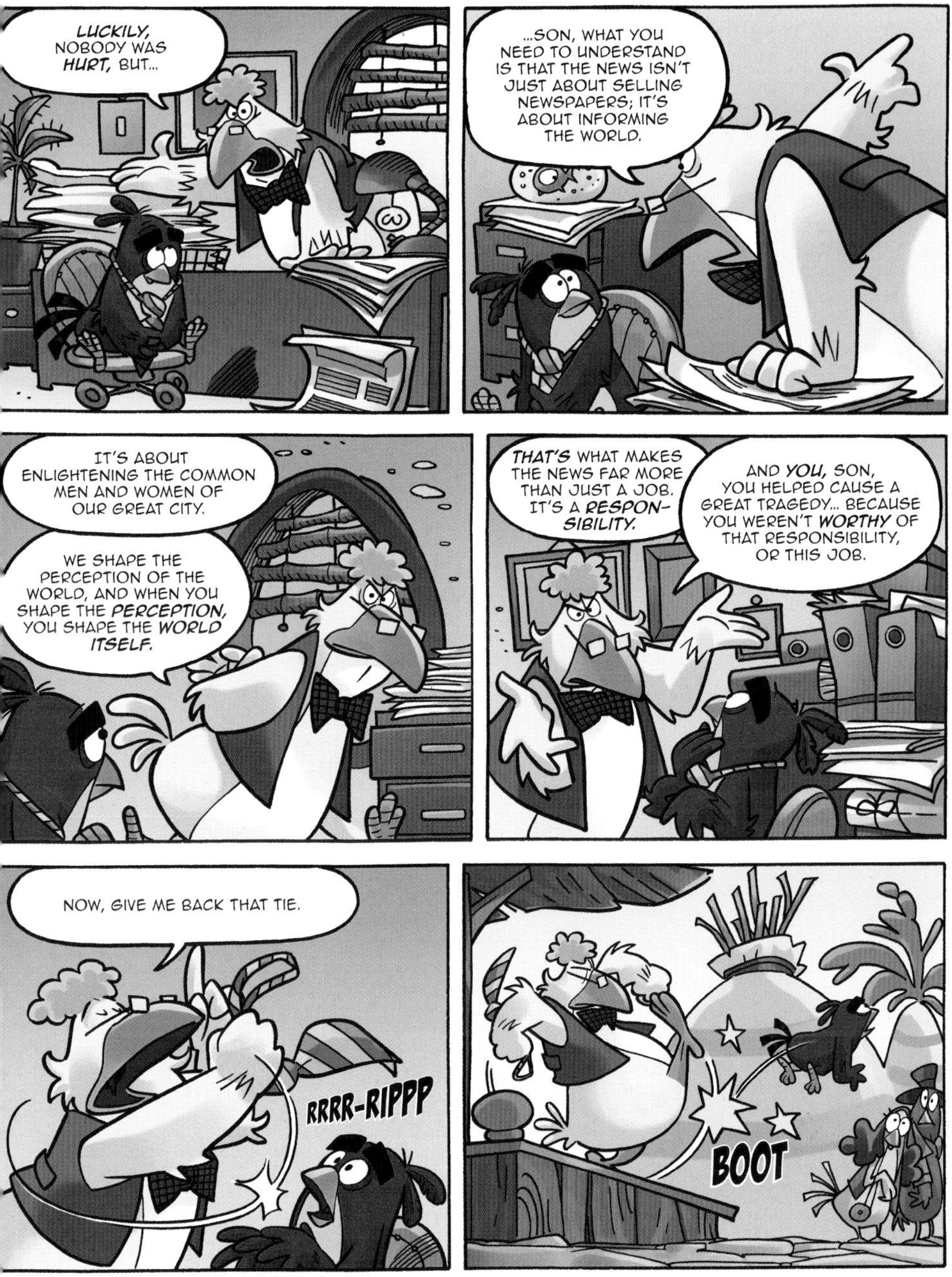

LUCKILY, NOBODY WAS HURT, BUT...
...SON, WHAT YOU NEED TO UNDERSTAND IS THAT THE NEWS ISN'T JUST ABOUT SELLING NEWSPAPERS; IT'S ABOUT INFORMING THE WORLD.
IT'S ABOUT ENLIGHTENING THE COMMON MEN AND WOMEN OF OUR GREAT CITY.
WE SHAPE THE PERCEPTION OF THE WORLD, AND WHEN YOU SHAPE THE PERCEPTION, YOU SHAPE THE WORLD ITSELF.
THAT'S WHAT MAKES THE NEWS FAR MORE THAN JUST A JOB. IT'S A RESPON-SIBILITY.
AND YOU, SON, YOU HELPED CAUSE A GREAT TRAGEDY... BECAUSE YOU WEREN'T WORTHY OF THAT RESPONSIBILITY, OR THIS JOB.
NOW, GIVE ME BACK THAT TIE.
RRRR-RIPPP
BOOT

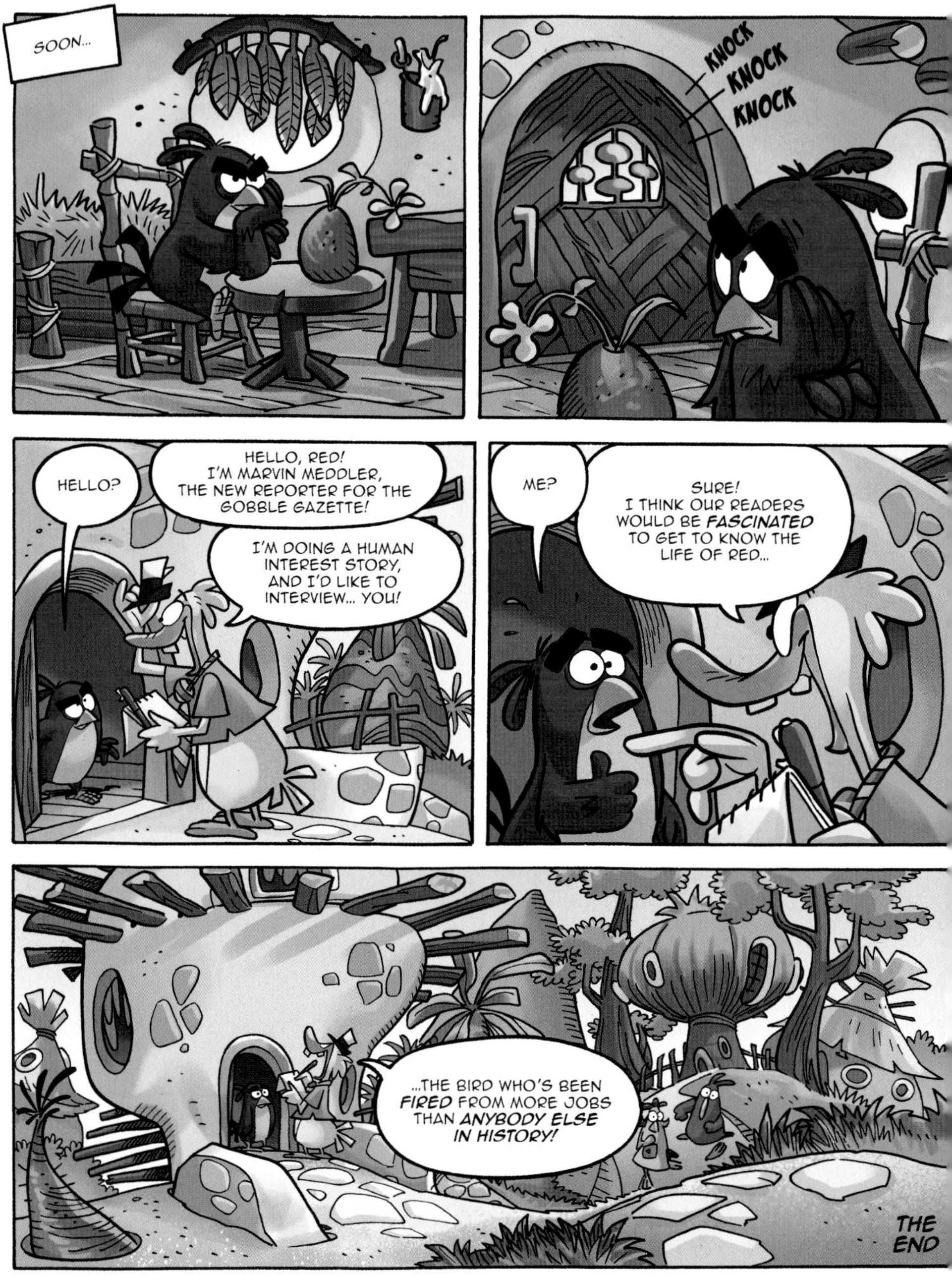
SOON...
KNOCK
KNOCK
KNOCK
HELLO?
HELLO, RED! I'M MARVIN MEDDLER, THE NEW REPORTER FOR THE GOBBLE GAZETTE!
I'M DOING A HUMAN INTEREST STORY, AND I'D LIKE TO INTERVIEW... YOU!
ME?
SURE! I THINK OUR READERS WOULD BE *FASCINATED* TO GET TO KNOW THE LIFE OF RED...
...THE BIRD WHO'S BEEN *FIRED* FROM MORE JOBS THAN *ANYBODY ELSE IN HISTORY!*
THE END

RED in... THE HOT AIR BALLOON

ANGRY BIRDS™

ISN'T THERE ANYTHING YOU CAN DO?

WAAAAHHH! I WANT A BALLOON WHY CAN'T I HAVE A BALLOON I WANT A BALLOON WAAAAAHHH!

BALLOONS

SORRY, MA'AM, BUT THE TANKS ARE ALL OUT OF GAS. GOT NOTHING TO PUT IN THE BALLOONS.

BALLOONS 1$ EACH OR 2$ FOR 3!

CAN'T BELIEVE I GOT A PARKING TICKET! #@*$! GOT KETCHUP ON MY SHIRT! ARGHH! AND THAT SANDWICH WAS WAY TOO EXPENSIVE!

URGH! EVERY- THING'S MAKING ME SO MAD TODAY!

SOB

BALLOONS 1$ EACH OR 2$ FOR 3!

?!!

THOOMP!

FWOOP!!

??!?

HERE YA GO!

YAAAAY!!!

SCRIPT BY **PAUL TOBIN** · ART, INKS, & COLORS BY **DIANE FAYOLLE**

THE END!

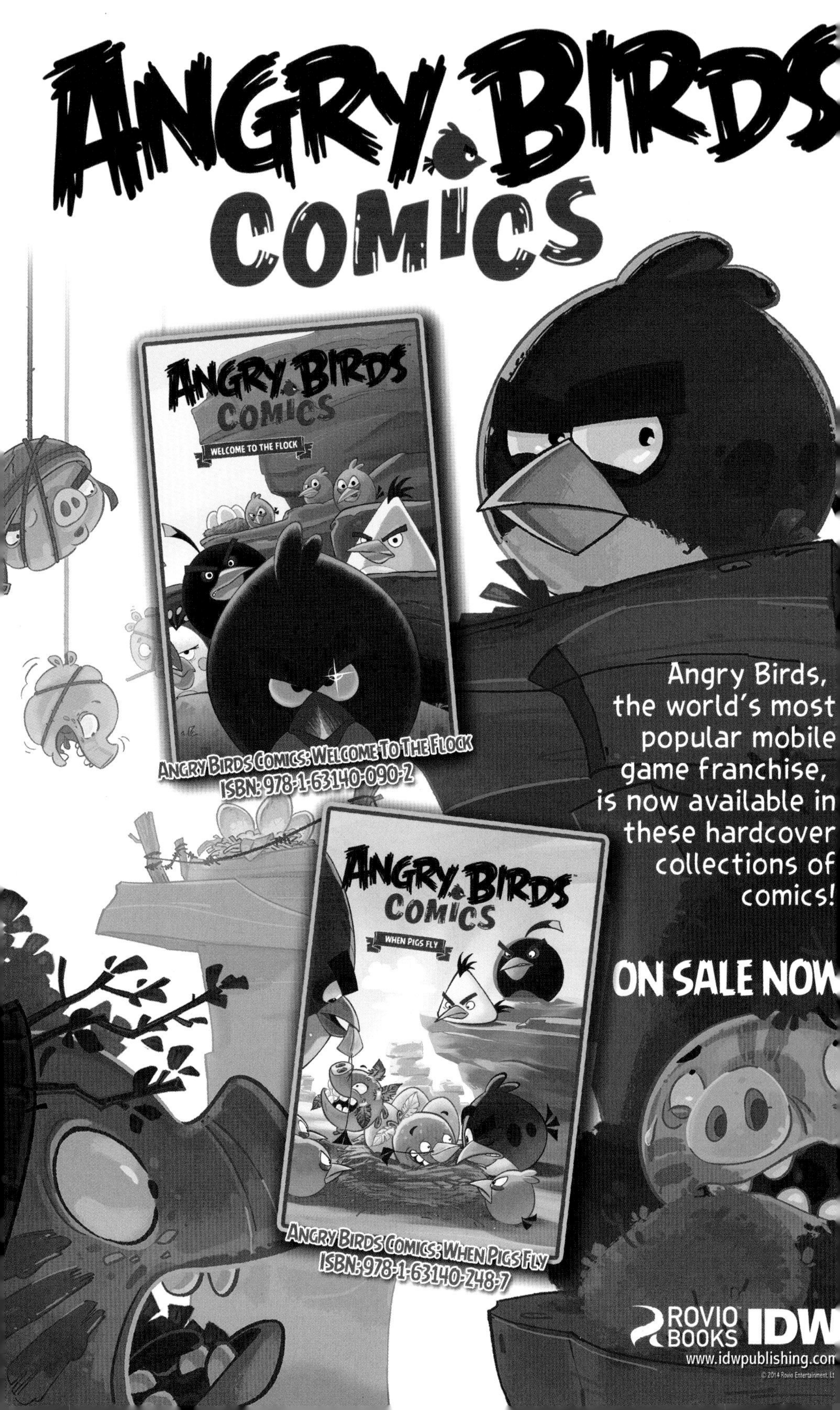

ANGRY BIRDS
COMICS
ANGRY BIRDS
COMICS
WELCOME TO THE FLOCK
ANGRY BIRDS COMICS: WELCOME TO THE FLOCK
ISBN: 978-1-63140-090-2
ANGRY BIRDS
COMICS
WHEN PIGS FLY
ANGRY BIRDS COMICS: WHEN PIGS FLY
ISBN: 978-1-63140-248-7
Angry Birds, the world's most popular mobile game franchise, is now available in these hardcover collections of comics!
ON SALE NOW
ROVIO BOOKS
IDW
www.idwpublishing.com
© 2014 Rovio Entertainment, Lt